The Girl Across the Pond

William Evans

For Suzanne

Author's Note

This book is a work of fiction. The names, characters and incidents are products of the author's imagination. Any resemblance to actual events or locals or persons living or dead is entirely coincidental.

William Evans

Author

Contents

Preface

This fictional romance follows an American soldier returning home from World War II after falling in love with an English girl. He has a girl back home waiting for their planned betrothal, yet he has no memory of her. Thus, he still loves the girl across the pond.

This tale of amnesia will span twenty-five years and intertwine with several lives along the way. It is a who's who of paramount proportions.

Does the combat soldier's memory return? Will he marry his lifelong sweetheart, or will he return to the girl across the pond? You will have to read further to find out. Along the way, plan to be entertained with suspense, humor, nostalgia, drama and did I say suspense?

Following this tale of romance, take a look at the author on the back page.

Foreword

If you liked 'An Affair to Remember', you will love 'The Girl Across the Pond'. Bill has realized a lifelong dream in writing this intriguing romance novel. After putting off his desire to write while pursuing a business career and helping to support his family, the time suddenly just felt right.

Bill has managed to incorporate everything you need for a true love story; an accidental meeting between a combat weary soldier and a beautiful young English girl, an instant attraction during the most romantic period in our history, a deep seeded love and intense passion.

The story contains humor, intrigue, unfaithfulness in a most unique fashion and a surprise ending that will engage both young and old alike.

While this is Bill's first novel, we can only hope it will not be his last. The Girl Across the Pond is a most enjoyable "page burner".

Ron Van Gilder

Houston, Texas

Chapter 1*France

He lay there covered in bandages, his vision blurred and a ringing sensation in his ears. He did not know how long he had been there or why for that matter. The last thing he remembered was being in an army jeep driving through a town in war-torn France seated alongside another soldier, a long legged Texan with whom he had become as close to as one could in war-time.

The explosion killed staff sergeant Henry Wilson instantly and threw the young lieutenant from the jeep and into a field, badly injured and with loss of hearing from the blast that took the life of his companion.

The Red Cross brought him to the hospital in nearby Paris which held many of his troops suffering from earlier confrontations with the Germans.

It was June 7, 1945 and the Allied Forces had taken France a day earlier. He was to have been flown to New York by army air transport the following month and then mustered out of service following four years six days active combat duty. That trip would have to wait.

***

He could not hear the staff hovering over him, nor could he see them all that well. His skin was burning from the shrapnel and his mouth was dry from thirst. He could not remember his name. All he could remember were those last few moments with his driver even though he could not remember his driver's name. He went back to sleep.

***

Both his vision and his hearing started coming back after a few days. The doctors told him what had happened and of the loss of his driver. His jeep ran over an old mine which blew the jeep off the road killing the sergeant and badly injuring him. He had lain there for days thinking about the sergeant and wondering why he could not remember the sergeant's name or anything else including his own name.

"Lieutenant!" The doctor startled him. "How are you feeling?"

"I feel tired," the soldier answered "and my head hurts."

9

"What is your name?"

"I don't know, sir."

"Do you remember anything before coming to this hospital?"

The soldier scratched his head and answered with a bewildered expression, "I remember the soldier next to me in the jeep, but I don't remember anything before that. Doc, why can't I remember my name?"

"Lieutenant, your name is Jason Alexander." Hesitantly, the doctor asked, "Lieutenant, do you remember home or your parents or where you went to school?"

"No, sir, I don't," he said with a whisper suddenly realizing his past was a complete blank.

"Do you remember anything at all?" the doctor continued.

"No, sir," he sheepishly answered and then went back to sleep.

***

The days and weeks passed with no progress as far as regaining his memory. However, his wounds healed and his vision and hearing were restored. They were simply a repercussion from the roadside bomb. He was thankful for that at least. Doctors determined that when he was thrown from the jeep he landed on his head causing the amnesia. As to the extent of the amnesia they did not know. It could be temporary or it could be long term. They were just not sure.

In the event this was a permanent condition the army wanted to send him on a little R&R (military slang for rest and recuperation) to England before shipping him stateside to see experts in the field. It would do him some good and give him time to prepare for the strangers awaiting him at home.

***

Home was in a town of just over 12,000 in Connecticut where he had gone to high school, was captain of the football team and met his sweetheart Amy Van Horn. Amy was cheerleader, homecoming queen and the daughter of Mr. and Mrs. Robert Van Horn of Van Horn Industries in Manhattan, NY.

Mr. Van Horn pioneered his company in his youth and had watched it grow from five employees to seven hundred employees in just ten years. His company was on the New York stock exchange and he was board member of several corporations.

Life was good for the Van Horns.

Robert and Elizabeth Van Horn were looking forward to their daughter's forthcoming wedding to her returning war hero. At least, he was a hero in her eyes. She and Jason had gone through high school and college together, fallen in love and planned their lives together. Then Uncle Sam paid Jason a visit. All Amy could do was wait for Jason's return. It turned out to be over four years. The only problem was, Jason would not remember her, as Amy would soon discover.

***

The chaplain asked Jason to sit down. He wanted to let the lieutenant know about his family and fiancé back home in Connecticut. Chaplain McCormick had pulled Jason's file and contacted the young man's family to let them know of their son's recent injuries and more importantly his memory loss. The family, of course was traumatized by the news.

"Lieutenant, I have talked to your family and gathered some information that I feel, and your family feels you should know."

Jason squirmed in his chair feeling uncomfortable that this man knew more about his family than he did.

"Your name is Jason Alexander. You live in Easton, Connecticut. You are an only child. Your mom and dad are both living. You graduated University of Connecticut, you played football and right out of college you were drafted into the army. Your dad owns the local newspaper, your parents belong to the local country club and you are a very popular young man back home, especially now since I told your dad about your getting the purple heart. Your dad's name is John and your mom is Susan and they love you with all their heart."

Jason gladly received all the information, but with a little reluctance. He was nervous about going home and meeting these strangers that were so much a part of his life.

"Jason, there is one more thing," Chaplain McCormick said with a long pause, "you are engaged to a young lady named Amy Van Horn."

Jason sat up straight with his eyes focused on the chaplain, and asked him to repeat what he just said. The chaplain repeated himself and Jason slumped back into his chair and let out a gasp of air.

The chaplain continued, "You and Amy were high school sweethearts, went to college together, played golf at the country club together and made plans to spend your lives together. Your country needed you first, however."

Was this really happening? Jason wondered. *Can I possibly go home and marry someone that I don't even remember?* His mind was doing cartwheels. He got up from his chair, saluted the senior army chaplain, thanked him and headed for the door.

"Lieutenant, take the R&R the army is offering you and get to know yourself. By the time you get home you may have a handle on this uncommon situation."

"I will, Chaplain. Thank you for your advice."

Chapter 2*England

London had not yet recovered from the blitzes of German Luftwaffe. It would be years before normalcy returned to this battered mega city. Jason wanted to get away from the reminders of war all around him and find somewhere warm and peaceful in the countryside. At least in this country he could speak their language. There shouldn't be a problem finding his way around. He could relax, do some sightseeing and discover himself as Chaplain McCormick so graciously put it.

He asked the cab driver to take him an hour away from London until he could no longer smell the residue of the large city behind him.

An hour later, the sky was clear, the air was fresh and for the first time since he awakened in the hospital he felt right with the world.

Now, if only I can find out what I like and dislike while I'm here.

He had arrived in a small town that looked pleasant enough. *Maybe I will uncover my personality with the strangers I meet here to prepare myself for what is waiting for me at home?*

They pulled in front of a medieval hotel that seemed harmless enough. He decided to get a room and explore the village.

***

There were no more visible scars and the young lieutenant looked very handsome in his uniform the next morning as he wandered from shop to shop in the village. He was naturally dark skinned. Some thought he was of Italian heritage, but the name Alexander defied that notion. He was solidly built from his days on the football field with a small waist, large shoulders and a smile that warmed the hearts of many young ladies when he was just a teen.

He spied an inviting café just across the street and took a step from the curb. A young woman not seeing him step in her path ran her auto into him and knocked him to the pavement. Fortunately, she was slowing down to park in front of one of the local shops and the collision was minimal.

She jumped anxiously from her car and reached down to help him, fear spreading across her face. "I didn't see you soldier! Are you okay? My God, where did you come from? I never saw you."

He could barely get a word in.

"Calm down, lady. I am alright. You barely hit me. Sorry lady, it was my fault," he said never looking up.

"Here, let me help you up," she started. "Are you sure you are okay?"

"I'm sure." He stood and brushed himself off. His leg hurt, but he had received worse hits from tackles and linebackers than that. Of course, he did not remember those hits.

"At least let me buy you a drink," she offered. "I want to make sure you are okay. Will you let me do that?"

Why not, he thought as he got his first look at her. *She was beautiful*, not as in film star beauty, but with a natural wholesome beauty. But then, he had nothing to compare her to since he could not remember women from his past. The only women he could remember were the nurses at the hospital.

This woman was tall, about five foot nine he figured and slender built with better than average breasts that curved upward like ski slopes.

Funny, how could I know about ski slopes?

Her hair was long and wavy with bangs swooping across her forehead. Her skirt fit tightly to her average size hips. She wore high heels which made her closer to his size. He figured that he must be six foot or more. He was actually six foot and one inch.

It was a quaint café where one could have a cup of tea and biscuit and a casual conversation. Of course, this was not the sort of biscuit he was accustomed to. A biscuit in England was a cookie. This would be a nice start to learning about himself in the presence of a young woman.

How would he handle himself with this stranger? Would he be able to speak intelligently about every day topics? Don't worry about it, he thought. *Just be yourself, whatever that is and let her control the conversation.*

They spent the next few moments introducing themselves. She was Maggie Ackerman, school teacher, twenty-five and single. She had graduated from Cambridge with a degree in elementary education and came home to Torrance where she had grown up and found work fairly soon as a teacher in grammar school. With a Cambridge education she certainly could have found work in a major school district in London, but she was a simple small town girl and this is where she hoped to marry and raise her kids.

Jason told her in the simplest way he could of his injuries and his memory loss and his reason for coming to her hometown. She was intrigued with his story.

She asked if he was married, but did not pursue with a follow up about a girl back home. After all, they were just meeting for the first time and although she relinquished personals about herself, she did not find it necessary to go any further with his personal history.

They seemed to hit it off very quickly. They laughed and exchanged pleasantries and enjoyed several biscuits with their tea. Jason found her very entertaining. They must have spent an hour talking. It was late July and school was not yet in session, so she had plenty of free time on her hands. What better than to show a

19

liberator of freedom the sights and sounds of her world and at the same time help prepare him for his return to his family and friends.

This will be exciting!

"Let me show you my fair city while you are here. What do you think?" she blurted out.

A huge smile crossed his face. "I would love that! How nice of you to offer."

"It would be my pleasure", she assured him.

Off they went and the rest of the day was like any other day for Maggie except that she was in the company of a very handsome young man and she rather enjoyed his American mannerisms which were so different from the young men she had known in her country. There had been boy friends in college and one young man back home after college that she had seen occasionally over the past four years, but nothing ever very serious. This man intrigued her and she felt something when she was with him that she had never experienced before. He was very physical in appearance, very proud, educated and with good common sense. He seemed to have it all together despite the absence of memories from the past.

She found herself growing very fond of this stranger from America and was keenly aware that this was not the norm for her. *Why am I feeling so close to this man? I have only known him for a few hours.*

She showed him the town library, the local grocery store, the school where she taught, the police station and most of the places that seemed important to her in this little community.

Jason was starting to feel the same connection as Maggie was feeling and liked the way she suddenly took his hand as they walked along the town's main street.

They went back to her car and she drove to the coast. They were east of London and the sea was just a short drive. They spread a blanket down on the beach and sat back to enjoy a moment of solidarity.

The sun was setting behind them. It had been a special day for both… for Maggie because he seemed so different than the others and for Jason because this was like a first date for him having no recollection of past relationships.

He wanted to kiss her, but is that improper with such a short friendship? Little did he know that soldiers had been kissing the European girls for the past month in record numbers since the Allied Forces took command. Then, while he was still considering the move she suddenly leaned over and kissed him gently on the lips.

His heart pounded and he now had the courage to respond. They kissed again and again as the sun slowly found the other side of the world.

Chapter 3*Lovers

She picked him up at his hotel the very next morning. She could not wait to see him. It had been a restless night for the both of them in anticipation of being together again the following day. He took a bath, shaved, dressed in his uniform and skipped gleefully down the stairs of the hotel like a teen with a schoolboy crush to meet her in front of the hotel in her waiting car.

They wanted to spend the entire day at the beach with a picnic basket and a bottle of wine that Maggie brought from home. He kissed her through the driver's side window and hurriedly went around getting in beside her. He was not sure if he could still drive.

Interesting, this amnesia. I appear to be able to do the most common things and carry on a normal conversation. I just can't remember the past. Most likely I can drive.

They would have two whole weeks together. He did not want to think about going back to France and she did not want to think about it, either.

Live for the moment, they both thought.

They drove again to the sea and laughed all the way as they entertained each other with clichés common to each of their countries. She called him a Yank and being the first time he remembered ever hearing that name he broke into laughter.

"The Civil War ended almost a hundred years ago, Maggie," he laughed. *Interesting, I remember the Civil War?*

She responded with laughter realizing Yank was a term given by Europeans to American dough boys and if he could not remember his past he certainly was not familiar with that term.

They shared the picnic spread and a bottle of French wine and added an occasional kiss. The sky was clear, weather perfect and Maggie and Jason were falling in love very quickly as did many war-time lovers. She asked if he wanted to see her home. He nodded and they returned to her car and headed back toward town.

***

She was renting a small cottage just a few miles from town that sat alone on two acres with a creek running through the property. She loved flowers and they were all around the house and in vases throughout each room. The home was well kept and she was proud of the way it looked.

She told Jason to have a seat on the sofa as she went into the kitchen to prepare a light meal for the two of them. She brought him a glass of red wine and went back to prepare an old family recipe of her mom's. Jason admired the way her home was decorated. It surely had the women's touch. He glanced at the photos sitting on the mantle over the fireplace which were evidently her mother and father. There was another photo sitting on a small table next to the sofa of apleasant looking man about Jason's age.

He would not ask about it.

They had a delicious meal. Maggie shared some more stories about her childhood and her family and they returned to the sofa for another glass of wine. Jason asked if she could play some music. She walked over to the turn table and placed a record over the spindle. The sound of Ella Fitzgerald began to surround the room. Jason loved Ella and all the romantic sounds that were available in the mid-forties.

"I see we have a common interest in music."

"Oh, I love American music," Maggie replied.

Jason reached over and kissed her gently on the mouth and she returned the kiss. Their lips grew wider and they pressed harder with each passing moment. Maggie was doing everything she could to suppress her feelings, but it had been a couple of months since she had shared her bed with another man and the temptation was overpowering.

Jason picked her up and carried her into her bedroom where she unlocked all her hidden passions. The night would be a turning point in both of their lives.

***

The next morning as they were leaving to take him back to his hotel he took her into his arms and said,

"Whose girl are you?"

"I'm your girl, Yank."

"And don't you forget it," he grinned.

26

After that, they made it a point to be together each day and night. They did not wantto waste a single moment while Jason was there. Their love grew and their desires grew as well. She had been with another man, pictured in the photo on the table, but it was purely physical and nothing more, for her anyway.

The man felt otherwise. He lived in London and she had put him off the two times he called by telling him she did not feel well.

***

On this day, she would take Jason to meet her parents. Lionel and Margaret Ackerman were middle-aged, born and bred Brits having spent their entire lives in Torrance. He worked at the local post office and she took in garments for alterations. They only made a moderate income, so it was through strategic planning and resolute savings that they could put their Maggie through college.

The Ackermans owned a small acreage similar to Maggie's that was outside town as well. Maggie lived there until she graduated and got out on her own.

They were so excited to see their daughter bringing a young soldier up the walk. She had never brought a gentleman to their home.

"Mum and Dad, I would like you to meet Jason Alexander who, as you can tell is an American G.I. and he is here on R&R which is an abbreviation for rest and recuperation.

"Well, hello Jason on R&R from America," her dad kidded.

"Welcome to our humble abode."

"Hello, Mr. and Mrs. Ackerman. I'm very pleased to meet you. You have a marvelous daughter."

"Thank you for saying that Lieutenant," responded Lionel who had served in the First World War and was familiar with rank.

"Well, don't just stand there you two. Come in and tell us what brings you."

"I just wanted you both to meet the man I care deeply about. I know, you haven't even heard about him. That is because we just met two weeks ago, but you know when it is the right one and we both just know. We can't stand to be away from each other for a moment. It is that bad."

"Well, glory be," declared her dad. "We didn't think you would ever find a man to suit you. This must be quite a lad."

"Yes, he is, Dad. He is the love of my life and tomorrow he is leaving me for America. But, he promises to come back for me. I know he will."

"Well, if he doesn't, I will go and find him," laughed her father.

"I will be back, sir. I love your daughter with all my being."

"How about you, Jason?" asked her mom. "Have you ever been in love?"

"Yes, I have, ma'am." He was actually telling the truth even though he did not remember the girl. "But," he continued, "I have forgotten all about her."

Maggie could not help but giggle.

"What is so funny?" her dad asked quizzically.

"It's a long story, Dad. I will tell the both of you another time."

"Well, come on in and we will prepare you kids something to eat," her mom announced.

29

The evening went well and both parents appeared to have a liking for their daughter's new beau. Jason told Maggie he felt right at home with them. This was a good beginning for a long relationship.

It was time to leave. Maggie's parents bid the young man farewell and wished him a safe trip home. They hoped it would not be very long before he returned. The two were eager to get back to Maggie's home and have another night alone. It would be a very memorable night to say the least.

***

As the two week adventure was coming to an end, Maggie felt compelled to ask where she stood in Jason's life plans. She told him that she loved him. She could not believe she said those words which she had never spoken before and especially to a man she had just met less than two weeks ago.

Jason responded with the same words, but there was hesitancy in his words. Maggie noticed and asked him what was wrong.

"I have told you about the amnesia and about not remembering my family and friends, but I need to tell you something else." He paused, wiped his forehead and began again, "I am engaged to a girl in my hometown. We grew up together, went through school together and evidently fell in love. I am told that we are engaged to be married."

Maggie pulled away quickly with a startled look on her face. There was a moment of silence as she struggled to maintain her composure.

"Why didn't you tell me this?" she questioned.

"When we first met and were exchanging information about one another, I didn't feel like it was important. We were just acquaintances at the time. Once we started sharing feelings for each other I blocked her out of my mind. I mean, I don't even know what she looks like for heaven's sake!"

"And now? What about now? You still don't know what she looks like and yet you are going home to marry her?" The first tear came to her eyes.

"No," Jason blurted out. "I love you, Maggie. I will go home and spend time with my family and find a way to tell her about us. Maybe after my four year absence she has fallen out of love with me, or maybe she has fallen in love with another man? Regardless, I will take care of the problem. It may take longer than you want, but you have to trust me."

They both just sat there holding hands, each with tears now.

"Let's make the most of the time we have left," Jason insisted. "It will be okay. Just wait and see."

She smiled and put her head on his shoulder.

***

They spent their final evening together at her cottage. They mostly held each other and spoke very little while listening to some Sinatra. They would save their final talk for the trip back to London the next morning.

***

Maggie picked him up early at his hotel and they made the one hour journey back to the London airport. Instead of talking as planned they drove silently most of the way. Jason felt pretty confident about their situation while Maggie was less sure. *This girl had more than ten years with Jason and I only had two weeks*, she thought. *How can I compete with that?*

They embraced at the gate, both not knowing what to say. She simply said, "I love you". Jason responded, "I will always love you. Wait for me." He started toward the gate, turned slowly and asked,

"Whose girl are you?"

"I'm your girl, Yank."

"And don't you forget it," he smiled as he started for the plane.

That scenario of sentences would become their common ground.

The flight back to Paris was filled with questions. He had so much to consider before his discharge and return to his hometown.

Chapter 4*Discharge

Jason paced back and forth waiting to see the chaplain again. They had much to discuss. He wanted to tell him about his new friend and how much in love they were. He wanted the chaplain to tell him that it would be alright to go back home and break it off with uh…oh, yes…Amy.

I can't even remember her name. Maybe she has forgotten me as well? Wait, maybe she has a new boyfriend and this won't be a problem for either of us? Dear Lord, please help me, he prayed silently.

Chaplain McCormick asked him to come in.

"How are you, Jason?"

"I am just fine Colonel, sir," Jason dutifully responded.

"Did you find it hard to meet with people or communicate with them while in England?"

"No sir, not at all. As a matter of fact I had no difficulties whatsoever. I surprised myself. Naturally, I hope to regain my memory, but as far as getting by and taking part in society I honestly believe that I will do just fine, sir."

"That is excellent," the chaplain smiled. "Is there anything personal you would like to share with me?"

There was a long pause…."Yes, sir."….another pause…."There is something I need to talk with you about. There is this girl." He stopped and smiled to himself just remembering her face. "I met this girl," he continued "and we seemed to connect right off and well, we wound up spending my entire two weeks together.

"Colonel Sir, we are in love and before you say anything let me assure you that it isn't just a war-time fascination. Sir, we connected in so many ways. We made each other laugh, we made each other cry, and we have so many of the same likes and dislikes. She is beautiful and pleasant and good and loving and funny and just so damn perfect, sir. Excuse me, sir!"

The colonel smiled at the lieutenant's exuberance. "Okay, lieutenant, what about your fiancé back home?"

Jason shuffled in his chair. "Well, sir, it has been four long years for her and just maybe she has found someone else, or maybe she doesn't love me anymore. You know, things change after a period of absence. I just want to go home and face up to it. We will go from there. Sounds like we were just matched together from the start and neither one of us gave ourselves a chance to look around."

"I hope so for your sake, lieutenant. If this poor girl has been sitting by the fireside for four years waiting for her true love to come home to her, I feel very sorry for your predicament; indeed I do and God help you if that is the case.

"On another topic, your mom and dad understand why you have not called them. They realize that it would be a difficult conversation for you to handle at this stage of the process. They are willing to wait until you get home and they pray that the sight of their faces will jar your memory. I pray for the same results, Lieutenant. Good luck to you and God bless you."

Jason rose from his chair and saluted the Colonel and thanked him for listening to him and being so understanding. He headed for his quarters to ponder the circumstances that lay ahead.

Chapter 5*Magic Carpet

The Army Department had planned for several years on how to move several million men and women back to the states at the conclusion of the war. Tents were set up for those waiting on demobilization. Various types of ships were used in this operation called Operation Magic Carpet. For example, the floating palace, Queen Elizabeth was used to take advantage of its size and speed. They crammed up to 1,800 men and women on the ship which consisted mostly of enlisted men with as few as 30 officers. This movement began in June of 1945, the month that Jason was injured.

He spent six weeks recovering and went to England in mid July. Fortunately Maggie was still out for the summer in July or their meeting probably would never have taken place.

The Queen Elizabeth took seven days to reach New York. Returning to France would mean a two week travel time round trip. It repeated this trip over and over along with aircraft carriers, cargo ships and various other vessels and aircraft. Jason was on the short list because of his amnesia. The sooner he could get back home to Connecticut, the sooner he could see specialists at the army hospital at Mitchel Field in nearby Long Island, NY.

He finally got the call to board on August 5th. His duffle bag was packed and his shoes were spit shined. He was eager to get home and settle everything with Amy. And, he wanted to take advantage of the American doctors at home. Yes, the doctors on base in France were Americans as well, but maybe they were not as familiar with his case as the specialists may be at home?

***

At last, here he is crammed like a sardine on a beautiful cruise line ship. Here he was just one of the boys. Nobody cared anymore about ranks, although they still saluted when necessary, but mostly everyone wanted to get back to civilian life away from the winds of war.

He was having chow with a few of the men and suddenly someone yelled his name. Jason looked up and noticed this officer heading toward him from another table with this huge smile across his face.

"Jason, what the hell are you doing here? We all thought you were dead!"

Jason reached out his hand to shake the stranger's hand, but the lieutenant gave him a big bear hug instead.

"You will have to forgive me. They tell me I have amnesia from a blast that took another soldier's life back in June and I can't remember anything from my past."

"Yea, we heard about the Sarg. Really sorry to hear that. So, I guess you don't remember me then?"

"No, I don't. I'm sorry."

"Hey, there's nothing to be sorry about, Jason. I'm just happy to know you are alive my friend! So, tell me what you have been doing, where you have been and don't leave out a thing. We have a whole week with nothing to do. Oh, by the way, I'm Forrest, Forrest McGuire. "

Jason filled him in on the details of the explosion and then asked, "Were we good friends?"

Forrest smiled, "We were best friends. I know everything about you and vice versa."

"Then, you must know about my fiancé at home?"

"Amy? Sure nuff, pardner," imitating their Texas friend. "You couldn't wait to get home and get married."

Jason frowned.

"What's the matter, Jason? Did something happen to her? Did she send you a Dear John letter?"

Jason hesitated and then began telling his new friend about Maggie. He told Forrest how much in love they are and the predicament he has found himself in. Now that he knows from this new found friend that he was anxious to get home to Amy, it makes everything that much more difficult.

"Tell me about her, Forrest. Tell me everything that I passed on to you. I need to know what she is like, what she looks like, what she cares about and what she dislikes....everything."

Chapter 6*Amy

Forrest had evidently paid attention when Jason talked. You could tell by the vast information that he began to pour out for Jason's brain to absorb. He described Amy as medium height, about 120 pounds, blonde wavy hair down to her shoulders, tiny waist, average boobs, decent hips and terrific legs.

She had a strong personality which she inherited from her tycoon father and an adventurous drive that came from her mom. She was athletic and laughed more than anyone in the room.

They had sex their junior year in high school and although he had nothing to compare it to he thought it was outstanding. She was always ready to give of herself and that was pretty often since Jason had strong urges himself.

They fought over little things, but never anything serious. She pretty much wanted things her way and he generally gave in to her whims. She wanted Jason to go to work for her dad when he returned home and keep her in the finer things of life that she was accustomed to.

"Did I ever tell you that I loved her?" Jason asked quizzically.

"Yes, you did, but you never carried on about it. I always felt like there should have been more expression from you when you talked about her. It just didn't seem like you were madly in love, if you know what I mean. You said that you were anxious to get home and marry her, but it sounded to me more like a planned event by both families that you were ordained to be a part of."

Jason looked confused. He put his hands behind his neck and leaned back in his chair to take it all in. *Wow!* He thought. *What have I gotten myself into?*

According to Forrest I may not have even loved my fiancé. How do I find that out? Do I start being with her again and see if she stirs emotions in me, or do I remain faithful to Maggie?

Chapter 7*Sarge

"Forrest what can you tell me about Sergeant Wilson?"

"One hell of a guy and one hell of a soldier! He saved your life, Jason."

"What?"

"That's right," Forrest confirmed. "It was during the Allied invasion of Sicily in forty-three, the Italian Campaign, it was called. We were on patrol. You were the platoon commander and Wilson was gunnery sarg. The Germans and the Italians were on their heels. An Italian straggler somehow got left behind in the retreat. You were with your communications man away from the rest of the company and virtually open targets. The Italian soldier came from your right with bayonet in hand and was about to plunge it into your back when Henry came out of nowhere and put a bullet in his head. You literally owe your life to that man.

He was asked how he happened to be in the right spot at the right time. His answer, "*I always kept watch on my company commander.*"

"God bless him," Jason said quietly.

The Queen was sailing into New York Harbor. It was early August. The Japanese would surrender within the next two weeks. However, since they were officially still at war, the G.I.'s onboard these transport ships could not radio ahead that they were coming home. They had to wait until they docked and find themselves a telegraph office, then send a telegram notifying their loved ones they were catching a train and would arrive on a particular date. That is exactly what Jason did.

His family was so excited. Amy was beyond herself. Everyone would be ready at the train station when he arrived for a grand reception.

Chapter 8*U.S. of A.

Jason waved farewell to his friend, Forrest standing on the train platform waiting for his train heading to Boston. The train ride to Easton should be so relaxing after the cramped quarters Jason had endured. It was not as hot for early August as customary. He would just sit back and enjoy the view with a cool drink.

As the train slowed for its arrival in Easton, Jason's heart palpitations could be felt beating faster and faster. He was to be met at the depot by three strangers…his mom, dad and fiancé.

He had requested that they not let the town folk know he was coming home. He simply was not ready for any kind of celebration. If not for that request, the entire population of Easton probably would have been there with a band playing.

The whistle sounded, the smoke cleared and the soldier walked down the steps leading to the pavement where he sat his duffle bag down and looked around for someone. He did not know what to look for except for a medium sized blonde in her mid-twenty's.

"Jason!" the woman yelled. "Jason, my son!" she cried out as Jason turned to see this rather attractive middle-aged woman racing toward him.

She held her arms out and he did not know what to do except embrace her. What else should he do? After all, this must be his mother.

She hugged him forcefully and kissed his cheeks over and over.

"My son, my Jason," she cried. "How are you my son?"

"I am great, mom...mother, err... what do I call you?"

"You always called me mom, son." She started crying realizing it was true that her son did not know her.

"Hi, son," his dad spoke softly as he reached out his hand. Jason took his hand and shook firmly.

My dad, he surmised. *What a powerful handshake!* He saw this tall, burly man with a beard and horn rim glasses and sporting a pipe. *He looked very distinguished as a newspaper man should,* Jason thought.

47

"Hello, Jason," a voice whispered from behind. It was a very sensuous and raspy voice. He knew it must be Amy. He turned around and there she was, just like Forrest described her. She was quite beautiful, indeed. He took a long breath.

"You're Amy."

"It's me, honey. It's your fiancé whose been waiting for four long years. And, I don't care if you don't remember me right now. I'm giving you a great big kiss anyway!"

She reached up and took his two cheeks between her hands and kissed him hard on the lips. It lasted for what seemed ten minutes.

Wow! He thought. *I should remember that kiss.*

They all just stood there staring at each other.

The ride home was filled with questions.

"Do you recognize anything about us?"

"Is my voice familiar?"

"Can you remember your school?"

Of course, Jason had his own questions.

"How long have you lived in the house we are heading to?" he asked his parents.

"Ever since you were in high school," his mom answered.

"What is the name of my high school?"

"Jefferson High," interjected Amy. "We went there together."

"I know. My buddy filled me in on the ship about you and me."

"What did he tell you about me?" she quickly asked.

"He told me how beautiful you are, that you have a great figure, an outstanding personality, and a desire for me to enter your dad's company. Should I go on?"

"Did he say anything derogatory about me?"

"Just that you usually got your way with me," he laughed.

They were coming to the high school and Mr. Alexander slowed down while Amy reminisced with Jason.

"I guess your friend told you that you were captain of the football team and I was cheerleader?"

"Yes, he did. He also told me that we went to college together at U Conn in Mansfield."

"That's correct. You received your bachelors in business administration and mine is in marketing," she said proudly.

"Sure wish I could remember those days. Guess we had a lot of good times along the way?" Jason sighed.

They pulled up to the home where he was raised. It was a typical small town upper middle class home with trees that shaded the front of the house from the afternoon sun and a swing on the front porch. It was very inviting and warm, just what Jason expected.

Inside was just as warm and filled with family photos. Although, theirs was a fairly small family there were plenty of frames sitting on various tables and the mantle over the fireplace. Amy's photos were in several places alongside Jason's and his mom and dad's were placed side by side as well.

Jason could not wait to sit down to that first home cooked meal. Nobody had to tell him that his mom was a great cook. He just knew she would be. The table was already set for four. Mom knew he would be hungry and she was anxious to place the Hungarian Goulash on the table and hope for a glance from her son that said he remembered.

The goulash was wonderful, but the glance did not happen, at least not for the reason she hoped for. But, he did give her a glance of appreciation. He was enjoying this meal more than one glance could tell her.

They made him feel right at home. Funny, when he thought of it that way, this is his home! He can not remember any of it. *I can't wait to see the doctors here,* he thought.

He would wait to talk with Amy about the change in his life regarding Maggie. This was not something he could just lay in her lap on the first day. It would probably take a couple of weeks before he could find the right moment. He also needed to see just how much she loved him and how strongly she still felt about marrying him.

***

The doctors at Mitchel Field were ready to see Jason. They had received his medical records and had spent time discussing the pros and cons of his amnesia. Jason wanted to go alone to the army base on Long Island. Amy argued, but this time she did not get her way. He said he needed the time on the train to think about the things going on in his life. He was absorbing so much information so fast and wanted some space.

***

Drs. Mickelson and Harris greeted Jason in Dr. Harris's office. They were both knowledgeable in causes and effects of amnesia and had seen cases similar to Jason's before. They were anxious to hear about his time at home with family and mix that information into the equation alongside his two weeks in England for them to be able to give him details on his particular type of amnesia.

Jason described how he seemed to know how to do just about anything he tries and things like catching a train and doing the math when he was presented a food bill on the train came naturally to him.

After about an hour of talking followed by a quick examination the doctors agreed that Jason most likely had Source

52

Amnesia. This meant that he could remember how to do things that he had learned in the past, but could not remember the source from where he learned them.

"For example," Dr. Mickelson said, "you can probably go right into the business world with your educational background and know exactly what to do regarding the course of studies you took part in at school, but you wouldn't know where they came from. Of course, yourfiancé reminded you of U Conn, otherwise you would not have known that is where your skills came from."

Jason felt so much better now knowing that he could probably drive a car, handle a bank account, play golf and so many other things that he feared were forgotten. He was anxious to get home and tell everyone the good news. Of course, the bad news was that the doctors had no way of knowing if it was permanent or would only last a short period of time. Jason was just going to go forward and he was so glad that he still remembered Maggie.

Maggie. Wonder what she is doing right now?

***

He arrived back at the Easton station where Amy was waiting. She came running toward him as he stepped off the ladder.

53

It was a scene right out of a movie, he laughed. *I shouldn't be laughing. She seems serious enough.* He did his part, subconsciously remembering a scene out of an American film he watched in Europe and opened up his arms and hoisted her up off her feet.

What am I doing?, he grumbled at himself. *I am encouraging her for heavens sake. If I am going to make a break with her, I have to be a little more reserved.*

She kissed him like there was no tomorrow.

Chapter 9*Bob and Liz

"You need to come over to Mom and Dad's house tomorrow, honey," Amy insisted. "They are so anxious to see you."

"You said, mom and dad's house. Do you no longer live at home?"

"Baby, I am twenty-five with a great job. I have my own place over in Summers Landing. I would have you over tonight, but I know you need to spend time with your folks. Naturally, I am dying to have time alone with you."

"Okay. How about you pick me up after ten in the morning and we can go pay them a visit. I'm looking forward to meeting them. Remember, I don't have any memories of them."

"I will see you in the morning. I love you," she whispered in his ear.

"You know I can't say those words back to you right now. I don't know you. Sounds strange, I know, but we just have to face it and take what comes."

***

Amy arrived early and the Alexanders invited her to stay for breakfast. Susan had made pancakes for Jason. There were plenty to share with Amy.

After breakfast Jason kissed his mom and told her he would be home later in the afternoon. His dad had already left for his office in town.

"It is so great to have you home, son."

"I'm glad to be home, Mom."

***

Jason and Amy arrived at the grandiose home of her parents in Highland Park where many of the elite from Wall Street and a few film stars lived. Her dad built thishome five years into his business and never looked back.

Mom and dad were waiting in the living area for their daughter and their future son-in-law. Mr. Van Horn arose upon their entrance and extended his hand to Jason.

He was a rather large man with thinning hair on his temples and none on the top. He started balding in his forties. He had a large belly and when he laughed, the belly rolled up and down. He probably stood six foot two if standing tall, but slumped over slightly which made him more like six foot.

"Proud to have you home, soldier. You have made the whole town proud."

"Thank you, sir. I'm glad to be here and looking forward to getting to know you and Mrs. Van Horn again."

Mrs. Van Horn started to cry.

"There, there Mother," Robert said to his wife of nearly thirty years. "No need for tears. The boy will be just fine. Soon, we will be right back where we were before this dastardly war."

Elizabeth was in better shape than her husband from daily workouts at the gym and tennis with the ladies in her bridge club. She loved Robert not only as a dutiful wife, but also as an admirer of someone who has excelled as Robert had in his many years in business.

Jason walked over to Mrs. Van Horn and shook her hand with one of his hands and patted the top of her hand with his other hand to console her.

"Like your husband said, ma'am…everything will be just fine real soon."

She smiled and hugged him.

They sat down and Elizabeth poured tea. Jason immediately thought of Maggie and England.

"Jason, my boy, what are your plans?" Mr. Van Horn quizzed him.

"I don't really have any at this point, sir. I just want to spend time with my family and friends and of course spend time with your daughter."

"Good idea, Jason. Just take your time. There's no rush. We can talk about your future later."

Jason knew what he was referring to. He had been told by Forrest of the plans to bring him into the company in New York after the marriage to Amy. This was all going too fast and he did not have a clue as to what to do next. Amy seemed to still be in love with him and it was going to be harder than he thought to break the ties.

They sat and talked for a couple of hours. Elizabeth made them lunch and afterwards Amy excused herself and Jason with an explanation that they needed some time together alone.

***

They drove toward Summers Landing and Amy's apartment. Now it was truly getting serious. Jason's mind was spinning thinking up ways to avoid having sex with her.

I can't believe what I am saying to myself. She is probably great sex! But, I love Maggie. I have to be strong. Oh, dear Lord, please tell me what to do.

They arrived at her apartment and Amy looked over at him and smiled. He didn't recognize that smile, but it was a signal that she used to give when she wanted him.

You're in trouble now, boy! he said to himself.

They walked hand in hand to the door and she unlocked it and followed him inside. It was beautifully decorated with the finest furnishings her mom could afford. Amy made good money, but Elizabeth still smothered her with the finer things she had grownaccustomed to growing up as a Van Horn.

"Can I pour you a drink?" she smiled again.

"Yes, I think I am going to need it," he said wryly. "Make it a double."

59

She fixed him a double bourbon and coke, his favorite she remembered.

"That's great," he commented after taking a drink…the doctors told him that he would still have the same likes and dislikes. "What is this?"

"That, my love is your favorite…Jack Daniel's black label and coke."

She cuddled over next to him on the sofa. He continued to sip his drink. She began kissing his ear. The perspiration was beginning to form on his forehead. She pulled his face toward her own and kissed him tender at first, then harder and longer until he had to pull away and take a large gulp of his bourbon.

"What's the matter?" she said in a little girl voice. "Playing hard to get?"

She took his empty hand and laid it on her breast. His pulse doubled. He needed another drink.

"Can I get myself another bourbon?" he asked as he jumped from the sofa. He hurried over to the bar and took his time mixing the two liquids.

Help me, Lord. I am being serious now. I am only human, You know. Of course You do. You made me.

He turned around and made his way back to her side and again she started pursuing him. She was so pretty and he was so excited.

Well, what's a man to do?

Her bedroom was very feminine with numerous pillows on the bed and little stuffed animals. She quickly brushed them to the floor and rolled back the covers. This man did not stand a chance…

It was still 1945 and Amy had to keep up appearances. It was getting late and time for her man to go home. Good girls do not let men stay overnight in small town America.

He had mixed emotions. He just had terrific sex with a beautiful woman and he felt guilty as hell.

I wonder what Maggie is doing? Is she sitting home waiting for my letter telling her when I am coming back? Oh, my

God, I feel so ashamed. I need to tell her something soon. I can't just let things go on like this. Maggie. Sweet Maggie.

***

Amy called early the next morning. "Darling, you were wonderful last night! I can't wait to see you again."

"I will see you tonight, Amy. I need to spend some time with my folks. Dad is going to take the day off at my request. We just want to sit back and visit."

"I understand, baby. I will call later. I love you."

She needed to get some work done, anyway. She had taken the week off to be with Jason. Since she was not going to be with him today she would catch up on personal business.

"See you, soon," Jason replied.

***

He wanted to tell his mom and dad everything. He needed them to know what he is going through and possibly they could help him get through this. But first, he would try to get a feel from them on their thoughts about Amy.

Did they love her? Were they really happy about the proposed marriage? Do they believe we are suited for each other?

If they were not as thrilled about everything as the Van Horns maybe it would be a little easier for him to tell Amy about his Maggie.

He really liked Amy and last night was outstanding, but his heart still longed for the girl across the pond.

Chapter 10*Surrender

It was August 15, 1945. The surrender of the Empire of Japan was announced by Imperial Japan, but the formal surrender would not be until September 2nd.

Jason heard the horns honking in the streets and people yelling out of windows. It was 9:00 p.m. Connecticut time. Jason and Amy were relaxing on her patio staring at the stars on this clear August night.

Now, the war was truly over. Germany, Italy and Japan were defeated and the world could get back to living in peace. Glory halleluiah!

The phone rang. It was for Jason.

"Isn't it exciting, honey?" his mom shouted into his ear.

"Yes, Mom. We can hear the townsfolk shouting from their cars. I feel so good for all my comrades in arms still over there. I was told by a good friend onboard ship that we lost a lot of buddies in Europe. I read that many more were lost in the Pacific. So sad."

"Just wanted to hear your voice, son."

"Thanks, Mom."

He still could not say he loved her, either.

He had spent the entire day with her and his dad. They shared a great deal of stories about his past both in Europe and from his youth. The stories of Europe came from the many letters he had written to them during the war. He never did get to ask the truly important questions.

"Let's celebrate, baby!" laughed Amy.

"I believe we celebrated just an hour or so ago," he joked.

She had manipulated him into her bed once again. This time was easier. He was setting his conscience aside for the time being and trying to convince himself that it was alright because he knew Amy in the biblical sense way before he knew Maggie.

Something about Amy was starting to connect with him. The many years they were together were surely helping him to feel some of the love they had. Little things were becoming normal to him, the way she laughed, the way she fiddled with her hair when they were talking.

He didn't remember any of that, but he related to it just as the doctors had described. This was just making things more difficult.

***

The surrender was profoundly important to Maggie. She would no longer worry about her kids. She often thought of a German invasion and what she would do to protect those innocent lives. Then, the Japanese were spreading their empire and she worried that they as well may come to England's shores.

She so wanted to talk to Jason and share this wealth of joy with him. But, she realized he was in an environment where he had so much on his mind and so many people to get to know again. He would call when he caught his breath.

The phone rang. It was Leslie Chapman, her long time friend and companion who had proposed to her on two different occasions. He lived in London in a high-rise apartment. They shared a lot of interests and they shared her bed, but she just never felt with him what she had felt with Jason. She wished that she did because Leslie was a really fine gentleman with all the right credentials. He was nice looking, but not ruggedly handsome like Jason. He was polite, courteous and always took her to popular places. He went out of his way to make her love him. It just was not in the cards.

"Hi Maggie. It's Leslie," he spoke in his distinguished English voice.

"Hello, Leslie. How are you?"

"Well, I am free for a couple of days and would love to see you if you are feeling better."

She thought for a moment...*I can't do any harm by going out with Leslie. Why not? Maybe I will tell him about Jason? No, silly girl, you have to wait until you get the call or the letter that tells you everything is going to happen just as you hope it will.*

"Okay," she answered. "What do you have in mind?"

"I just want to be near you. I don't care what we do. Why don't I just drive down and we will play it by ear?"

"That will be fine." *Why does he have to be so sweet?*

Chapter 11*Must Tell

Jason decided to give it one more shot. He was going to tell them straight out how he had fallen in love with an English girl and he could not get her out of his mind. He needed their guidance and wisdom to help him get through this. He really did not want to hurt anyone.

He sat down in the living room with both parents. He had asked his dad for a bourbon and coke. He was sitting there idly stirring the drink and contemplating how to start.

"You look concerned, son," his dad said. "What's troubling you?"

"Dad...Mom, I need you to know something. I am in a very difficult situation and hopefully you both can be my sanctuary.

"I was sent to London for some R&R after the doctors thought I was well enough to be on my own. They wanted me to find out what it was like to be amongst strangers and unfamiliar settings to see how I would handle it. They hoped this would benefit my journey back to the states.

"While in the London area I met a young woman. She was just trying to be helpful and show me the sights and we connected immediately. She was pretty, not as pretty as Amy, but with a more inner beauty. She laughed all the time. She was smart, but not in the way Amy is. She kept it hidden, but you just knew it was there. She was nice, not brash as Amy can be. She made me feel like I was the only man alive."

He took a breath as his parents looked quizzically at each other.

"We continued to be with each other for the next two weeks and fell madly in love with one another. I can't explain it. She just fits my need. That is the only way I can explain it. I think about her constantly…even when I am with Amy.

"I told her I would be back after settling things here, but Amy keeps pulling me in to her web and I don't know how to escape. I sure don't want to hurt her."

John and Susan just leaned back in their respective sides of the sofa and let out a sigh.

"Oh, Jason. This marriage has been planned for over four years and both families knew from your teens that it was meant to be."

"I know, Mom," Jason agreed.

"Her dad has plans for you in his business," she continued. "Amy has sat back and waited for four years for you to return. You couldn't have a more faithful fiancé. She gleams when she is around you. She simply adores you.

"This just breaks my heart," she sighed.

"What do you have to say, Dad?"

"Son, you have so much vested in this relationship. You have a lifetime of memorieswith Amy and…" he stopped himself. "Sorry, I forgot. You have no memories, but both of ourfamilies do and I feel like we would not be having this conversation if you had not been injured.

"I am sure this new you really and truly loves this girl…"

"Maggie, Dad. Her name is Maggie."

"Yes, Maggie, and I'm sure she is a fine young lady, but you have to access the real world right now and get back to reality.

Use common sense which should tell you that this would not be happening except for the amnesia."

Jason listened intently. He knew that his dad was right, but his heart was telling him to ignore everything his father was saying.

His mom chimed in, "We both love Amy, son. And, you loved her as well before the bomb. Our families have grown up together and there have been so many plans made which include you and Amy. Please give it a lot of thought."

Again, he knew his mom was right. Common sense tells him that this is all a result of the blast that took away his memory. *Do I go along with everyone and just hope that I fall back in love with Amy? Yes, she is gorgeous. Yes, she is great in bed. Yes, she is educated, smart, funny and popular among her friends. And, my future is probably set if I go to work for her dad.*

I just need to be alone.

Chapter 12*Parade

Jason decided to catch a plane for Dallas and visit the family of Henry Wilson in nearby Garland, Texas. This trip was two-fold, console the family of the man who saved his life and have time away from family and Amy to think through his circumstances. He needed to tell Maggie something very soon.

***

His plane landed in Love Field in Dallas. He had never been to Texas, but even if he had he probably would not have remembered anything about it.

He took a cab and told the driver he wanted to go to Garland. The driver told him it would be an expensive cab fare. Garland was about twenty miles. It was a small town of about 5,000 where everybody knew everybody.

Football was king in Garland, so if you knew someone that played football for Garland High School you could write your own ticket.

Jason had done his homework on Henry and knew he had played tight end for the Garland Owls. With those long legs, he could reach over all the corner backs and catch passes thrown his way. He led his team in touchdowns all three years at Garland.

Jason had the address of Henry's parents. He hoped they would be home. They did not know he was coming.

He had worn his uniform hoping it would be easier for a stranger knocking on their door to be welcomed. He knocked on the front door.

Henry's parents knew immediately this must be a friend of their son.

"Sir, my name is Jason Alexander and I was a friend of your son." He tipped his hat to the woman standing next to Henry's father.

"Please come in, Lieutenant," the father smiled. "We were hoping a friend of Henry's would pay us a visit. This is Henry's mom. There is so little we know about his last few months overseas."

They took seats in the small living room.

"I was with your son when the jeep ran over the mine."

"Oh, my God!" exclaimed the mother as she put her hands to her mouth.

"I was thrown from the jeep and landed on my head and suffered amnesia. I could not even remember your son's name. They had to tell me in the hospital. I later found out from another officer that your son and I were good friends even though I am an officer and he was an enlisted man. There was a very good reason that we became friends. He saved my life in Italy."

The Wilsons held each other. Jason reached out and held their hands and thanked them for having such a fine young man for a son. He told them the story of what happened in Italy. They listened intently as Jason talked about their son the hero.

"The town is going to have a parade in his honor tomorrow right down Main St.," Mr. Wilson proudly told Jason. "Will you still be here?"

"I wouldn't miss it," Jason smiled. He had discovered this information in his research and thus planned to be here for the ceremony.

"We would be proud to have you stay in Henry's room tonight. It would give us comfort for you to be here."

"I would be honored, sir." He was wondering where he would find a hotel or motel in this small a town.

***

He awoke to the smell of fresh coffee, bacon and eggs with homemade biscuits and gravy. He ate every bite on his plate and then some.

The parade would start at noon in the town square. The parents were to ride in a Cadillac convertible. Mr. Wilson made a call and Jason was invited to join them.

It was heartwarming to see so many people turn out. Everybody knew the former football hero and in a small town word spreads fast. They all knew about Jason.

At the end of the parade, there were a few speakers including the mayor. He asked Jason to join him on the podium and introduced him as Henry's commanding officer and friend.

It was a very humbling day.

***

Amy picked Jason up at the airport and they went straight to the club where they both played golf as kids. Jason was starving and anxious to see his old stomping grounds.

It was a typical small town country club with the stone gate entry, the circle drivethru and the one story white clubhouse.

It was early September and the grounds were very green and manicured. Jason wondered if he would be able to play golf being without any memory of playing.

They enjoyed a fashionable lunch on the patio in back of the clubhouse overlooking the course.

"Do you remember anything, honey?" Amy asked as she finished her after dinner drink.

"Sorry," he replied.

He looked at her closely. She was very radiant this afternoon. Her hair was pulled back in a pony tail. She had on a white golf outfit. She appeared very athletic.

I like that look, he thought. *I actually like everything about her. I just don't feel anything. I still love Maggie. It doesn't make any sense. Maggie and I only had two weeks together. Why can't I feel that way for Amy if we shared those feelings for so many years?*

He was baffled.

I have got to make a decision. It has been over a month since I last saw Maggie. I need to write her and give her some idea of what is going on, but I don't even know myself. What can I say to her?

He felt so guilty sharing Amy's bed since being here, but how on earth would he explain not wanting her? What man turns down a woman that he knows was his love in a former life? She would not understand. He had never turned her down before. It would just force him to tell her about Maggie and he was not prepared to do so. He would takeanother couple of weeks and let this scenario play out.

Chapter 13*Decision

Another week went by. Jason and Amy met with some old friends and he had to endure the same conversations over and over about what happened to him and why he did not remember any of them. It became very monotonous.

They also spent several more evenings at her apartment and the final result each time was not so monotonous, unfortunately for his conscience.

The thing was, he was beginning to feel closer to Amy each time. She wasn't the soft, gentle woman that Maggie was, but she had something special just as Maggie did. There were dramatic differences in the two women, but a man could find solace from either of them.

***

Amy asked Jason when they were going to set the date. Now, it was crunch time. He knew it and Amy knew it. They were mid-twenties and needed to get started with their plans to spend life together as a family. In the forties, women thought they were old maids if they had not married before thirty and started families.

Jason sat alone in the back of his mom and dad's house staring at the sky. He was looking for help from somewhere.

"Dear Lord. Tell me what to do," he asked.

He started putting everything into perspective, his parents, Amy's parents, extended family and long time friends…and of course Maggie and Amy.

It was really not as complicated as he had originally thought. Yes, he loves this English girl with every fiber in his being, but when placed alongside his entire family, friends and common sense, he felt there could be no other decision than the one that would make Maggie very unhappy. He must go through with what was supposed to be. There were emotions here much larger than his for Maggie.

He must write that letter.

Dearest Maggie;

I have missed you so much. It has been quite an ordeal for me to come home and deal with all the forgotten past and the plans that were set in stone for me and my fiancé.

I truly thought it would be easier than it has been because I love you so much, but there are so many loved ones involved and so many hearts that could be broken by my decision.

With the strongest regret that I can possibly make to you, I must tell you that my life must go on as forecast prior to my amnesia. It is breaking my heart to write this letter. My love for you is so strong and I do not feel the same for Amy. You have to know that.

I pray that you can accept this decision as one that has multiple rationalities. One day we will both realize my decision was for the best. It may be one sided, since I know it is totally unfair to you, but knowing how strong a person you are, I can find justification in what I amdoing and simply hope and pray that you find happiness without me in your life.

I love you with all my heart. May God bless you and keep you strong.

Jason

Chapter 14*Pregnant

Maggie read Jason's letter and she felt her stomach tie into knots. She knew this was a possibility, but continually prayed for the best. This was a dagger to the heart, one that she did not know if she could ever get over.

She had a good long cry. She was all alone with no one to lean on. *What would she do now? How would she cope with this life changing event?* Like Jason said, she was strong and time would heal.

***

She missed her time of the month several weeks ago. She tried not to think about it and kept her mind on hearing from Jason and on her kids at school. They kept her comforted while waiting to receive news from him.

Now the letter had come and she remembered. It had been seven weeks since that first time with Jason. What if she were pregnant with his child? Should she write him back and give him the opportunity to change his mind?

Dear Lord, what am I to do?

She had to make plans quickly. She was a school teacher and school teachers in 1945 just did not get themselves in a way that she has found herself in. Her career would be ruined.

Leslie would marry her. He has asked her plenty of times. She could tell everyone they married during the previous summer while she was out of school. The townsfolk all knew of their relation. And, she had not seen any of her friends or acquaintances while with Jason.

This would work!

But, wait…would Leslie even consider marrying me while carrying another man's child? He and I have not slept together in probably three months. He always wanted to, but I was not as anxious as him since I did not love him. Therefore, he would surely know that it could not be his.

I will just have to tell him about Jason and see what happens. Oh, my. He may never want to see me again.

She called Leslie in London and told him she wanted to see him. They made plans for the next evening. She would prepare one of his favorite meals, have a candlelight dinner and a few drinks and then at the right moment tell him about her brief encounter.

***

Leslie arrived early. He had longed to see Maggie for the past couple of months. She had continually put him off with one excuse after another and he was beginning to wonder if it was over.

She greeted him at the doorway with a gentle kiss. He hugged her and told her how much he had missed her.

Dinner was magical, he thought. *She looked radiant and there was a glow to her face that he had not seen before.* He told her so.

Of course, Maggie knew why her face was glowing. *Isn't it true that this happens when you are pregnant?*

They moved to the sofa with their drinks and got comfortable. He was wondering if they would wind up in her bed tonight. He longed for her. It had been on his mind a lot lately.

He loved her so much, but he was the perfect gentleman and did not push her. She never really told him that she would not marry him; she simply told him she would think about it.

She was moving up in years and there had been nobody to come along until Jason that ever interested her. She really liked Leslie, but just did not love him the way she always knew she wanted to love a man.

"Leslie, you know how much I like you. I have never told you that I love you because it just was not there for me. You know that. You have always known that. I don't believe I ever led you to believe otherwise."

"I know," he replied softly.

"I told you I would think about it when you would propose to me, but deep in your heart you knew that I only said that out of respect for you and your goodness and your kind heart. I believe you always knew that I might possibly marry you simply because you love me so much and knew you could make me a good husband."

"That is true, Maggie. I have always known that there was something missing and I just hoped that it would grow over time. What are you trying to say?"

"This is probably the hardest think I have ever had to say to anyone," she started.

Oh, my God. She is going to break up with me!

"Leslie, I have done something that I am totally ashamed of and it breaks my heart to have to tell you…you the last person that deserves this.

"While you were in London and I was telling you that I wasn't well, I was seeing another man. We just happened to meet in town and we connected. One thing led to another and we spent two weeks together.

"We fell madly in love."

Leslie's heart sank into his stomach. He had never expected this.

"There is more. I let him into my bed and now I believe that I am carrying his child. He told me that he had a fiancé back home in America, but that he was going to go home and break the engagement and come back to me."

Leslie was in total disbelief.

"I received a letter yesterday from him informing me that for many reasons that are complicated he was going to go ahead with their marriage plans. I don't have to tell you how broken hearted I am, but of course that is not something you want to hear."

Leslie could hardly breathe. There was total silence.

After what seemed several minutes Leslie took her hand.

"Maggie, I want to make an honest woman out of you. I want to give that child a name and I want to love you the same way I have always loved you without reservations."

Maggie started crying. She had prayed that he would do this and she was so glad it was his idea. That helped her to feel a little better about the circumstances.

"Leslie, you are the exact man I thought you were. No girl deserves you. I just don't know what to say to you."

"Just say, yes."

"Yes," she cried.

Chapter 15*Wedding

Jason knew Maggie had received his letter by now. He felt terrible, but realized he had done the right thing. He was ready to move on with his life and accept the fact that things were meant to be the way they were before.

He called Amy and asked her if she had plans for the night.

"Are you kidding me?" she laughed. "My plans are totally with you."

"Great! I will come over tonight."

One thing he could say about Amy, she was always vivacious.

***

He arrived just as the sun was sliding over the backdrop of Easton's miniature skyline. She was very casually dressed in shorts and halter top. She had her usual broad smile on her face and gave him her usual greeting, a big kiss on the lips.

"Do you want a drink?"

"Yes, I do."

She poured his usual bourbon and coke. He preferred Jack Daniel's black label, but would drink whatever was available.

They shared some small talk and she nibbled on his ear. The mood and setting were actually apropos for the proposal he had planned.

She even had Glen Miller playing on the turn table.

Jason sat down his drink. He stood up from the sofa, took one step toward her and got down on one knee.

She shrieked!

"Amy, I haven't even told you that I love you. However, you know my circumstances and I believe you will fully understand when I tell you that I realize now that this is what I wanted before the injury and it is clear to me that you still feel the same way that everyone says I felt prior to the war.

"So, with that entire mouthful out of the way, Amy, would you do me the honor of becoming my wife?"

"Yes, yes, and yes!" she repeated loudly and pulled him toward her where she could kiss him profusely.

He had gone to the local jeweler earlier and picked out a ring. He reached into his pocket and pulled out the tiny velvet box and opened it.

"It is perfect!" she stammered, "just beautiful!"

First she called her dad and mom to give them the big news. Next, they called Jason's parents. John and Susan were actually shocked, but happy about his decision. Their lips were sealed.

"You pick the date," Jason said.

"The sooner, the better!" she half shouted. "Right now, I think you know what I want to do," she giggled.

Yes, I do like her spontaneity, he thought to himself.

***

The date was set for the first Saturday in October which should prove to be a beautiful day in Connecticut. Both sets of parents got involved with as much as Amy would let them. She was as giddy as a school girl and Jason was glad that she was so happy.

He had located Forrest and his war buddy agreed to be best man. Amy chose college roommate, Grace to be her matron of honor. Grace had married two years prior. She would make a beautiful matron even though she was eight months pregnant.

The wedding would be at the All Saints Episcopal church that both had attended growing up in Easton. Amy told him that Father Jim was still the rector, realizing of course that Jason would not remember the Reverend. But, they would be meeting with him and let Jason have a chance to get acquainted again.

The reception would be held at the Easton Country Club.

Chapter 16*Wedding-2

"You are indeed pregnant, Maggie," the doctor confirmed. It was mid September.

Now, for sure she and Leslie would marry after knowing positively that she was having a baby. The baby should arrive mid April. That would be nine months since thatfirst night with Jason on July 16th.

She called Leslie and told him the news.

"Leslie, can we get married right away? We can tell people later that we eloped during the summer while I was off work. Let them think what they want to think. We can make up all kinds of reasons as to why we did not tell anyone.

"Of course darling, anything that makes you happy."

Leslie was ecstatic. He knew she never loved him, so nothing has changed and he was still praying for her to learn to love him. The baby was just icing on the cake in his eyes. He loved children and would make a terrific father.

Maggie took a day of vacation on Friday. They took care of licenses that day and on Saturday they drove to London where they found a justice of the peace and made their pledges to one another.

Maggie truly respected this man for committing himself not only to her but to her baby as well. Leslie was a remarkable man.

She let her mind wander just for a moment to remember Jason, but abruptly returned her thoughts to her new husband.

They spent the weekend seeing the sights of London such as they were after four years of war. They made love each night and she told him that she would try with all her might to learn to love him.

"That's all one can ask for," he smiled.

Leslie decided to move in with Maggie and drive the one hour commute to London rather than have her make that drive. She would tell her co-workers that she did not want to tell them she and Leslie were married until he moved into her home. Now that he had done so, she would tell them they were married in July.

Maggie was happy. She was looking forward to this baby and to her life with Leslie. She just knew it would be a good life. She hoped for nothing but the best for Jason and his fiancé who was still nameless to Maggie.

Chapter 17*Ceremony

Jason was nervous. His buddy was by his side and saying all the right things, but Jason still felt uneasy. He knew he was doing the right thing for everyone else, but was it the right thing for him?

Amy looked magnificent in her wedding gown. She stood in front of a full length mirror as the matron of honor and bridesmaids gathered around her. She was so happy.

The sound of the organ seeped through the walls of the church and the procession began. Amy's dad looked proud in his tuxedo. He held his head high and proceeded down the aisle. Amy could see Jason facing her as he stood alongside Forrest whom she had met the day before. *Jason was so handsome*, she thought. *What a lucky gal I am!*

The marriage went as planned. Father Jim performed the Sacrament of Holy Matrimony and pronounced the nuptial blessing over the marriage followed by the Eucharist. Communion was taken by all that were baptized. The formality of Peace was given and the bride and groom kissed followed by blessings from well wishers.

There was still more to the traditional Episcopalian ceremony with verses to repeat and hymns to sing. The complete ceremony was much longer than the protestant ceremony. Amy was anxious to get off her feet.

The wedding party headed to the club for a reception. The Van Horns went all out with the food and drink and decorations. There was a five tier cake for the bride and a three tier for the groom.

Amy and Jason took the floor while they played Sentimental Journey, a current hit by Les Brown and his orchestra. They were indeed a beautiful couple and appeared extremely happy to all attending.

Jason's parents looked on with a little bit of trepidation.

Amy's parents were as thrilled as they could possibly be. The dream had finally come to fruition.

Forrest made a toast to the couple. He spoke of the friendship he shared with Jason on the front lines in Italy and of the gallant leadership that Jason displayed over and over. He wished the couple happiness and beautiful children.

The guests all laughed.

The father of the bride announced that the offer still stood if Jason wanted it, a job with Van Horn Industries in Manhattan.

The father of the groom wished the couple joy and success in whatever they chose to do with their lives. He told them that he loved them very much and choked up trying to get the last word out. His wife patted him on the arm.

Chapter 18*Honeymoon

They chose Florida to honeymoon. It was October and Florida should be perfect. They stayed at one of the finer hotels on Miami Beach compliments of Robert and Elizabeth Van Horn.

Room service was the order of the day. They wanted as much time in their room as possible those first couple of days. The beach could just wait.

Amy was doing her best to make Jason a happy man and he was enjoying it thoroughly. There was one thing he was sure of; he loved sex with this woman.

"Let's take a break," she laughed "and go to the beach."

"I'm game," Jason agreed.

They jumped into their bathing suits and off they went.

The beach was white, the water was a deep blue and there was not a cloud in the sky. They took full advantage of the weather and lay in their cots, drank Pina Coladas and tried to get back their energy that was spent over the last two days and nights.

***

They went shopping for gift items for their parents and found several interesting items that should prove appropriate. They held hands like a couple of school kids and Jason was actually happy. He had not forgotten Maggie, but would put her in a special place in his heart that would remain private.

They danced at night, slept late in the mornings and ate everything in sight. The week ended way too soon.

They left Connecticut as husband and wife and left Miami as lovers.

Chapter 19*To Work

Jason sat down at Mr. Van Horn's invitation. They were in the study where they could have some privacy. Amy was in the kitchen with her mom practically bursting at the seams over anticipation of the results of her husband's and father's talk.

She knew what her dad wanted. It had been discussed time and again since graduation from college.

"Jason," Mr. Van Horn began. "You know what I have you here for. We have talked about it many times. But, let me tell you my new plans before we talk commitment.

"Since you have no memory, I will tell you about my company and of my new plans for the future which I hope will include you.

"We manufacture a line of women's fashion. Before the war we only had fashion shops in New York. We went by the name of Van Horn as opposed to Van Horn Industries which is the name of my manufacturing company in Manhattan. We supplied fashion to stores all across the U.S...

"Now, however, with the war over in Europe, I see a huge opportunity to expand to London and Paris. Those were the fashion markets before the war. I foresee a boom in the industry and my designers are working day and night to launch new post war designs not only for American women, but also for European women. I feel it in my bones. It is going to be huge!"

"That really sounds exciting Mr. Van Horn."

"Call me Dad. If you come to work for me you can call me Mr. Van Horn.

"Now," he continued, "I want you to be my liaison to the shops in London and Paris. I realize you know nothing about women's fashion, but you have education in business and from what you tell me about your amnesia you will retain that knowledge once you get into the field and begin to use it.

"I don't expect you to know anything about the garment industry or the fashions we produce. I just want you to be an overseer and public relations man. I want you to make sure the people I put in charge of the stores are doing their jobs and make sure the books are correct. All the store managers will answer to you.

"You will receive a five figure salary and bonuses if the stores prosper.

"Well, what do you say?"

"Wow, I am speechless!" Jason blurted out. "Dad, I mean, Mr. Van Horn, I accept your generous offer. When do I start?"

It was November, 1945 and Robert Van Horn knew in his gut that it was coming. By December of the following year designers like Christian Dior would become fashion icons around the world.

Van Horn was going to beat them all to the punch. Even with the constant strikes going on in New York just three weeks after the Japanese surrender, he felt confident. The elevator operators strike came first. Nobody realized how dramatic their strike would be. The city was at a standstill. There was no access to the offices in the towering structures of Manhattan other than climbing stairs.

Next came the garment industry followed by the tug boat captains. For over a year the city was reduced to about one-third of its normal gross national product.

It affected Van Horn Industries, but Robert kept enough crew onboard to start production for his overseas plans. While New York would struggle, European markets would thrive and especially in the fashion industry.

Amy had gone to work for her father after graduation. Her degree in Marketing would prove valuable to the company. She was especially gifted in her field and gifted as well with personality suited for her line of work.

She and Jason would be traveling in the same circles, but with different goals...hers to pursue business, his to manage operations. It was an exciting time in their lives.

* * *

Jason spent the next several months in his father-in-law's office building. The elevator operator strike eventually subsided as did the tug boat strike. Other strikes would come and go over the following two years making it the worst strike in New York history.

Meanwhile, Jason learned as much as possible about garment manufacturing, buying the materials needed, exporting to foreign ports and as much as he could about design. It wasn't

necessary, but would be helpful.

Chapter 20*Jonathan

Maggie was giving her class their homework assignments when she suddenly felt a sharp pain. It was the second week of April and she knew.

She sent little Johnny to the head master to tell him to send her a relief teacher. The Head Master came along with the relief teacher and volunteered to take Maggie to the hospital.

Off they went to the local hospital and within the hour she had delivered a seven pound baby boy. *Jason would love this baby boy,* she thought.

The baby was fine. The new mom was fine and daddy was in route.

He looked like Jason, she smiled.

Leslie arrived and was anxious to see how Maggie was doing. He almost ran to the nurse's station.

"Mrs. Chapman! Where is she?" he blurted out almost out of breath.

"Are you Jason?" the nurse asked inappropriately. "She kept asking for you in delivery. We were hoping you would get her soon."

Leslie was taken aback. He just nodded.

"Room 116 on the right."

Leslie felt his gut wrenching. He thought things had been better between them.

He walked into her room and she smiled at him. The baby lay cradled in her arms relaxing after having mother's milk.

"Are you okay, Maggie?"

"I am just fine now that you're here," she smiled again. "Here, hold him."

"It's a boy?" he asked as he reached for the baby.

"Yes, a fine boy with a head full of hair and all ten fingers. Say hello to Jonathan."

Leslie took the baby from her and snuggled him to his chest. "Hi, old chap. Daddy has got you."

Maggie smiled, but beneath that smile she was crying out for Jason.

Chapter 21*Vocation

Leslie Chapman had graduated from Cambridge with honors. He was sought after for his intelligence, his impeccable taste, his distinctive gentleman's mannerisms and his generally likeable personality.

Simply put, he was just one of the good guys. He dressed sharply and stood tall and elegant like a man of aristocracy.

He chose to be a buyer for London's largest department store. Like others, his travel time had been very limited upon the closures of fashion shops in occupied Europe. But, now there was talk of a comeback and he was excited to face the challenge.

Naturally, it would mean leaving Maggie for weeks at a time, but it was necessary to give her the type of living that they both wanted for their child.

Word was that fashion stores would be opening by late October in the two major fashion cities.

The baby had arrived in April. It was now early

October. That had given them plenty of time to get acclimated to the

new family life before his leaving the two of them on buying trips.

Maggie had taken leave the last two months of school and

along with the summer months had completely gotten back to

normal and was ready to return to work in September.

They were getting along beautifully. Their lives were full

with Maggie teaching and Leslie traveling back and forth to

London. They found a common ground in their marriage despite the

situation with the baby. He had promised to give the baby his

unconditional love and give it his name.

Maggie was growing fonder of Leslie each and every day

and admired the way he had taken command of their lives together.

They agreed to keep Jason out of their lives and would decide when

the child turned eighteen whether or not to tell him about his

biological dad.

Leslie had not gotten over her calling out for Jason in

delivery. *Would she ever love me?*

He needed love in his life. His upper crust look did not

defy his need for romance. Was he just going to accept this sexual relationship that tendered no true love? There was an overwhelming difference, in his opinion between sex and romance.

Maggie was really trying to be a good wife, but she could never make herself be romantic to a man that she did not love. She loved Leslie, but she was not *in love* with him.

Chapter 22*The Journey

Amy and Jason had been together now for one year. During that time she began to see that something was missing in her life. She had only known one man and that was Jason. He was her first and there were never any others.

Even during those four years he was away when she would have urges beyond her control she brought closure to them by spending time with family and friends.

Now, she had all the physical attention that she needed, but there was something else…something that she always knew she wanted but did not dwell on that much.

She wanted her husband to be a man of distinction, a man that was both elegant and commanding, and a man that was upper crust in society.

Jason was just the same guy she went to school with. He was a ruggedly handsome man with a laid back personality and somebody you would expect to see coaching a football team, not working on Wall Street.

She didn't want to over think the subject. She knew she could not make him over into what her vision of a perfect husband was, although she would try in small increments so that he would not be aware.

***

The Van Horn Fashion's stores were opened in October of 1946 in both European locations and Amy was heading to London for the grand opening. Jason would fly to Paris which would be the hub of their overseas venture.

Amy would do some marketing while in London as well. Much had been done via the phone to get things in production, but her face to face soliciting was badly needed.

Jason kissed her goodbye from their apartment. They planned on purchasing a home after returns from their first deployment.

She flew out of LaGuardia headed for the newly opened London Airport which was almost fifteen miles west of London.

She had made arrangements to stay at one of London's finest and looked forward to a good night's rest before venturing into the city streets.

***

She awoke early, showered and dressed in her best business attire. She then headed down the elevator to the hotel restaurant and bar for breakfast.

It was a relief to see elevators with operators.

The grand opening of her father's London operation was not until Saturday. She would take this opportunity to call on the head buyer at the largest department store in town.

***

She entered the giant department store and ventured through various departments admiring the displays. She asked one of the sales ladies to direct her to the store's offices. She was told to take the elevator to the sixteenth floor.

She stopped at the front desk on sixteen and asked for guidance to the merchandise buyer's office. She was told to take the elevator to the seventeenth floor.

111

The elevator door opened and she was facing a reception desk with a lovely young lady eager to help.

"My name is Amy Van Horn."

She would use her father's name to establish an inside track to buyers.

"Oh yes, Mrs. Van Horn," the girl said excitedly. Everyone in the business knew the name Van Horn.

"What can I do for you today?"

"I am here in the hopes that your head buyer is in. Would that be a possibility?"

"Yes, Mum," she said in her English curtsy.

She buzzed the buyer's office and his voice came over the speaker, "Yes, miss Donna."

"Mr. Chapman, there is an Amy Van Horn here to see you."

"Send her in, please."

Donna rose from her desk and asked Amy to follow her. Toward the back of the office floor was a large office with privacy blinds all around.

"Mr. Chapman, this is Mrs. Van Horn."

"Come in, Mrs. Van Horn," the gentleman spoke as he rose and buttoned his jacket.

"Let me offer you a seat."

"Thank you Mr. Chapman."

"Are you married to a member of the Van Horn family? I see you are wearing a wedding ring."

"You will have to forgive me, Mr. Chapman. I am the Chairman's daughter. I thought it would be easier to get in to see you if I did not use my married name."

"Very clever," he responded with a chuckle. "What may I do for you?"

"I'm sure you have heard through the rumor mills that our company has expanded to Europe and includes a store here in London."

"Yes, I have," he nodded.

"Well, naturally we would like to have your company's business. We have the grand opening this Saturday and I would like very much personally for you and your wife to join us."

"Actually, I was planning on going. I hadn't thought of bringing the wife, but that might be a good idea. She needs to see what my business entails. Thanks for the invitation. She will be excited.

"Listen, Mrs.? …"

"Let's just stay with Van Horn. I think it will be less confusing while I am abroad."

"Listen, Mrs. Van Horn, it is almost lunch time. Would you care to join me?"

"I would be delighted," she smiled.

She was still full from her breakfast, but would not turn down an opportunity to discuss business with the head buyer for the largest department store in London.

***

They sat facing each other in a busy pub directly across from the store. Ale was the choice of lunch for most along with a sandwich of which there were many varieties. She asked him to order for her and he knew exactly what to tell the waiter.

There was plenty of small talk while they ate. She was admiring this distinguished man who spoke beautiful English and with such elegance. He was handsome in a stately way and poised beyond his years, exactly the kind of man she had dreamed of.

"Of course, I am familiar with your company's pre-war fashion, but know nothing about your post-war designs. I am looking forward to seeing your collection on Saturday and maybe I will buy something for my wife."

"That is a tremendous idea, Mr. Chapman."

"Call me Leslie, please."

"Okay, Leslie, call me Amy."

They both smiled and continued to finish their meals.

He was catching himself thinking of this woman in other than a professional way, something he had not done since first meeting Maggie. This was a beautiful woman with a radiant personality and charm. She was so different from Maggie.

He needed to get his mind back to business.

They finished and said their pleasantries to one another and agreed to see each other again on Saturday.

"Oh, honey. That is a wonderful idea. I will leave Jonathan with mum and dad. After all, he is six months now. It shouldn't be a problem for them.

"I will wear that blue outfit you bought me the last time you went on a buying trip. You said you loved me in it."

"Good choice, Maggie. We will have a good time and you will get to see me in my element."

***

They arrived at Van Horn London in the heart of the fashion center. The store was beautiful. The neon sign was very sheik.

Van Horn Fashions

They entered and immediately noticed the crowd that had come to see this new line of American designed fashions for European women.

Leslie looked for Amy and spotted her over by the temporary bar that had been set up for customers during this grand opening.

"Maggie, let me introduce you to Mrs. Van Horn," Leslie said.

They walked toward her and Amy noticed this very lovely lady in an unassuming way coming her way alongside Leslie.

They do not go together, she thought. *He is much too debonair for her.*

"Hello, Mrs. Van Horn. Great to see you again," Leslie greeted her.

"It is so nice to see you again as well, Mr. Chapman. This lovely woman must be your wife."

"Yes, let me introduce you to Maggie, my wife and the mother of our child."

"Very glad to make your acquaintance Mrs. Chapman. Do you have a daughter, or son?"

"A son, Jonathan. He is six months old and we just left him for the first time with my parents. I miss him already."

"How delightful!" exclaimed Amy *and how matronly,* she thought to herself.

"Well, ladies. I need to look at the fashions. Why don't you two get to know each other?"

117

Leslie walked away and Amy offered Maggie a drink.

"Well, Mrs. Van Horn, Maggie started…

"Call me Amy, please."

"Well, Amy, I can't help but notice your wedding band. Is your husband the owner of Van Horn Fashions?"

"No dear, he is my father."

Maggie looked confused.

"I used my dad's name to get in to see your husband. It worked. I asked him to continue to call me by that name to avoid confusion while I am abroad. I merely want to separate my business world from my personal life."

"I totally understand," Maggie responded. Sort of a women's right thing, huh?"

"You might say that. How do you like our shop?"

"It is quite beautiful, Amy."

"We have a runway in the back where our buyers come to watch the lovely models parade across the stage in our finest," Amy continued. "We hope to set Europe on its heels with our new and more modern lines of clothing. Our designers have gone to great lengths to provide something for everyone."

"How excited you must be," smiled Maggie? "What does your husband do, if I may ask?"

"He is also with my dad's company. He is the operations manager for Europe which is London and Paris at this time. I guess that makes him my boss as well as my husband." They both laughed.

"Here, take another drink with you and let's see some of the designs," Amy suggested.

They strode over to where Leslie was standing and joined him in viewing the designs on the various racks.

"Shall we go to the runway and watch the ladies?" Amy asked.

"Oh, I would love to!" Maggie said excitedly. "I have always wanted to do so."

They followed Amy through a doorway and into a very large room with a small runway and several chairs for buyers to sit and study the ladies wear.

Amy guided them to a section where chairs were available and they sat down to enjoy the parade. Some buyers were there, but mostly this was a time for tourists and other shoppers to get a look at the future of women's clothing.

***

The opening was a success. Amy would have a good report for her dad and for her husband. Her marketing concepts were in place and evidently working. Her husband and father would be proud.

She wished she could have some more alone time with Leslie. She really liked this man and it was exciting to think of flirting with someone new. She had never been given that opportunity growing up since Jason was always the boy and man in her life.

There would be other times, she thought.

Chapter 24*Paris Store

Jason walked in with some trepidation. He had spent the past year preparing himself as best he could but still felt he was lacking in knowledge of the industry.

The store was busy with the bustle of buyers, shoppers and clerks. He asked the first clerk he approached where he could find the store manager.

"The gentleman over there with the silver hair, Monsieur," the clerk spoke in a French accent but with perfect English. Robert Van Horn had insisted that all store employees speak both French and English fluently.

Jason walked over to the man. "Excuse me, Monsieur, but I am Jason Alexander."

The gentleman perked up as if to military attention.

"My great pleasure Monsieur Alexander."

"Please call me Jason. No monsieur necessary."

"Very good, and the same with me Jason. My name is Pierre," responded the older gentleman in kind.

"So," Jason began, "It appears to be going very well, Pierre?"

"Very well indeed. I believe the new fashions introduced by your father-in-law are tremendous. He evidently has expert designers in house."

"What kind of feedback are you receiving?" Jason asked.

"The professional buyers are here from all around the world having heard of Van Horn Industries... how do you Americans say.... blazing a new trail in Europe. I feel sure the French designers will soon be following our lead."

"That is very good news, Pierre and you are so right about the French designers and Italian and others. The rumors are everywhere. New York is having problems now and the fashion industry is at a standstill, so Europe is ideal for the explosion of post war designs that we feel is coming.

"You surely know that I am brand new in this game and I hope I can depend upon your knowledge when I feel that I need it?"

"I am at your disposal Jason, any time."

The two men escaped the crowd for Pierre's office in back so that they could talk over the business aspect of the store. Jason would want to see how the books are set up, how Pierre is preparing for the possible onslaught of orders, get some feedback on the store personnel and anything else Pierre could tell him in general.

The butterflies were churning in his stomach. He was excited about his new business venture.

Chapter 25*Reunion

Six weeks had passed since the grand openings in London and Paris. Both were successful and ahead of the game as they say in America.

Little did they know of the coming of the great designers later that year. All Robert Van Horn knew was that he had launched a post war fashion that was intriguing to the European women. His designs were mostly for the mainstream woman. The wealthy were buying, but Van Horn Fashions was not a sensation with them at this point.

*****

It was November and Amy was due back in London. She had been to both major fashion cities and expertly marketed her product. She and Jason both had done well and dad was pleased. However, she and Jason had seen very little of each other.

It worked out this time that Jason was going to London as well. They would make a vacation out of the trip together.

She thought to herself, *I can't wait to see Leslie again. It would be exciting to have both men near me and execute my fantasies between the two of them.*

Naughty girl....she laughed.

***

They stayed at the same hotel that Amy had stayed in before. That way she would be close to Leslie's office and have a better chance of running into him. If not there, maybe at the store.

Why couldn't I just call him and ask him to meet us at the store? He probably needs to return by now, anyway.

She picked up the phone in her room and called Leslie's office. They put her right through.

"I'm so glad you are in town," Amy said with exuberance. "I want to invite you to come back to our store and meet my husband, Jason. If you remember, he is our European director of operations."

"I would be delighted to join you," he responded.

Jason...I detest that name, he muttered under his breath. *It must be a common name in America?*

"How about tomorrow at noon, Leslie?"

125

"Tomorrow works for me, Amy. See you there."

"Bye, Leslie."

***

It was the next morning over breakfast when Amy expressed how anxious she was for Jason to meet the head buyer for Harvey Wickham. She explained that Wickham was the premiere department store in all the British Isles and she had called on Leslie during her first trip.

***

Both Amy and Jason were in the Van Horn store when Leslie arrived. As soon as Leslie stood face to face with them, Jason recognized the face from the framed photo on Maggie's sofa stand more than a year ago.

He stared for a moment and then caught himself.

"Sorry, I thought you looked familiar for a moment. But that is impossible since this is my first time in London."

He had not told Amy of his R&R to London. The less she knew about him in 1945 the less chance of her finding out anything about Maggie.

126

"On any account, it is very nice to meet you Leslie. Is it alright to call you Leslie? I noticed that Amy did so."

"Yes, perfectly alright and you are?"

"Oh, please forgive me, Leslie," stammered Amy. "This is my husband, Jason. Jason Alexander."

"It is indeed a pleasure to know you, Jason. May I call you Jason?" I told your wife soon after meeting to be informal with me and the same goes for her husband."

"So, how long have you been with Harvey Wickham?"

"Eight years. It took me six of those years to become head buyer."

"I see you are a married man," Jason said looking down at his ring on the left hand.

"Yes, my beautiful wife, Maggie and I live in nearby Torrance. Almost a year and a half now," he smiled.

Jason's heart stopped. Of course, he knew that she would probably marry, but this means she married almost immediately after his letter to her. It hurt to know she acted so quickly. Maybe it was a marriage on the rebound?

He just had to see her again.

"We would love to meet her. How would you both like to join us tomorrow evening in the supper club at our hotel for dinner and drinks and maybe a little dancing? We are trying to make this a combination vacation and business trip. We would both enjoy having you join us since we do not know anyone here.

"Would that be alright with you, Amy?" Jason asked.

Amy was thrilled at the chance to get Leslie on the dance floor and do a little school girl flirting.

"Of course, it will be," she agreed.

Jason was beside himself. He was both excited and scared of what to expect when Maggie sees him. Will she give us away? I miss her so very much.

***

Jason and Amy went down to the supper club, both anxious for different reasons. This could be a very special night, or it could be a disaster.

Leslie and Maggie were escorted to their table by the maitre d'. Jason purposely had his back to the entrance.

He and Amy rose as the couple came around to the other side of their table. He raised his head and looked straight at Maggie. Her face flushed with shock. His face glowed with remembrance of days gone by.

She caught herself quickly as her husband began introductions.

"Darling, this is Jason and Amy Alexander."

Maggie responded as best she could, "Very pleased to meet the both of you," as she looked again at Jason with surprise in her eyes.

Amy extended her hand for Maggie's.

Next, Maggie reached out for Jason's trembling hand.

When they touched they could both feel the rush of blood through their fingers. He did not want to let go.

Jason forced a smile.

"Hello, Mrs. Chapman. I am so pleased to meet you."

"Thank you, Mr. Alexander."

"Please call me Jason."

"Jason," as she nodded approval.

Maggie was seated to the left of Jason while Leslie was seated to the right of Amy. The tension in both Maggie and Jason should have been noticeable, but Amy and Leslie were so interested in seeing each other again that they did not notice. They were caught up in their own little masquerade.

They ordered drinks and discussed a little bit of their home life both in London and in America. They shared simple stories like what there was to do in their home towns and what did each one like to do socially.

Leslie and Amy did most of the talking as Jason and Maggie stole a glance at one another as often as they could. He so wanted to touch her, feel her breath against his lips and put his arms around her.

Dinner was served and there was mostly quiet with the music playing in the background. They were playing some Glenn Miller. Jason and Amy approved.

Upon finishing their meal, Leslie asked if Amy would like to dance. She did not hesitate to accept and off they went without so much as a "By your leave".

Jason took Maggie's hand and placed his other hand over it and stared into her eyes. "Maggie, sweet Maggie. You look so beautiful. I can't get over it. You and I sitting here. It's just unfathomable."

Maggie's hand trembled. "Jason, what in the world are you doing here? Leslie told me we were meeting Amy and her husband, but of course I didn't realize who Amy was even though we had met last month and became friends. Oh, my God! This is just not happening. Why are you here? Did you ask to come with her from America in hopes to see me?"

"Well, that would surely be a possibility," answered Jason, "but the fact is I am the European operations manager for Van Horn Fashions while my wife is in marketing. We were both scheduled to be here.

"As soon as I saw Leslie, I remembered the photo by your sofa. I intentionally found a way to get us all together. I just had to see you.

"I am so glad I did."

"Well, naturally, I am too Jason, but weren't you taking a big chance?"

"I didn't care. I think of you all the time. Even though I told you in my letter that I discovered it was for the best; that did not take away from the love I felt and still feel for you."

"Oh, Jason. I still love you as well. I really do. I was so broken hearted. Leslie was always there for me and I just took advantage of him. He had asked me several times. I feel guilty because I love another man."

"Would you like to dance?" Jason proposed.

She responded that she would and he took her by the arm and headed to the center of the floor away from where Leslie and Amy were dancing.

He held her in his arms lightly at first so as not to bring attention to themselves. He watched over her shoulder for any sign of Leslie and Amy looking his way. He could feel Maggie's warm breath against his neck and the trembling fingers in his grasp. He wanted to put his lips against her cheek, feel the smoothness of her skin that he still remembered with fondness.

"I have never let you out of my mind and heart. Believe me," Jason spoke deliberately. "It was my intention to come back for you. You must know that."

"I believe you, Jason. It was just so hard for me to appreciate at the time and I needed something to take me away from the heartbreak. That is the only reason I married Leslie," she lied.

I want him to know about his son, but I just can't. I need to raise my son in a normal environment with no attachments of scandal.

"I understand, Maggie. Truly, I do. And, I feel deeply for the hurt that I caused you. I can imagine it because I felt the same hurt," he continued as he looked around for his wife and their new friend.

Amy was dancing rather close to her customer-friend-dream man. Leslie could feel her presence and rather liked it. He felt rather wicked for the moment and not ashamed. He was still hurting from the memory of Maggie calling out Jason's name during delivery.

There must be a lot of Jasons in America, he thought to himself again.

Amy drew closer and caught herself breathing hard on Leslie's neck.

What a charming man, she thought. *Wonder what he is like in bed?*

The song ended and both couples returned to their seats just as a Glenn Miller song was starting. Jason stopped and whispered in Maggie's ear,

"Whose girl are you?"

"I'm your girl, Yank," she grinned.

"And don't you forget it," he whispered.

"You two dance now," shouted Leslie over the music pointing to Amy and Jason. "That's American music at its finest."

"What do you say, Amy? Want to cut a rug?"

"Why not?" she responded as she wiggled toward the sound and headed out to the center of the floor.

Maggie watched with envy as the man she still loved moved very astutely across the glittering marble dance floor.

He was actually pretty good, she mused.

Leslie watched Amy as she showed off her skills opposite Jason. He liked what he saw.

Wonder what she is like in bed, he grinned.

Chapter 26*Christian Dior

Business was booming for the Van Horns, but there was a man on the horizon that would bring a whole new excitement to fashion. His name…Christian Dior.

Christian Dior, the name also given to his fashion store opened on December 16, 1946 in Paris to mixed reviews.

Initially, women protested because his designs covered women's legs, but eventually his fashion ideas drew rave reviews and re-established Paris once again as the center of the fashion world.

Van Horn Fashions was mainstream apparel for the most part while Dior mostly sold to the very wealthy. Robert Van Horn decided to get onboard and add a similar fashion to his established line. The entire fashion industry would benefit from Christian Dior's contributions to the fashion world.

Dior would be the first of many famous designers to appear on the fashion scene thefollowing year. Some had made their mark prior to the war and re-established themselves post war as did Jacques Fath and Pierre Balmain while some were thought to be Nazi sympathizers as was Coco Chanel who moved to Switzerland for a few years following the war before coming back into the scene.

Chapter 27*Affair

Throughout 1947 the industry was taking tremendous strides with the likes of Dior.

Jason and Amy traveled extensively throughout the year of 1947 trying to keep up with the pace. Amy had several opportunities to see Leslie both in London and Paris.

After spending time together on many occasions having lunch, or dinner the physical connection grew to a fever pitch while in Paris surrounded by the beauty of the city and the very romantic Parisians.

***

They had met in Van Horn Paris while Leslie was busy buying for his company. Amy asked him if he wanted to join her for dinner that evening and he answered "Yes" without turning from his conversation with the store manager. He was all business when the time called for him to be so. She would have to wait for him to be attentive to her.

They could both feel the connection growing tighter and each considered the consequences of taking advantage of those feelings. They were just being drawn together way too often to negate those feelings. Tonight would be a turning point in that relationship.

It was a higher than typical November temperature in Paris at fifty-two degrees, just comfortable enough for a stroll along the Seine river. Leslie told her of the scattering of ashes of Joan of Arc in 1431 into the Seine as they walked hand in hand under the moonlit night. Everything was just right for a romantic encounter.

They both could feel the temptation taking control as they continued to walk with the sound of the river splashing against the boulders lining the bank. Suddenly, Leslie stopped and took Amy into his arms and without any resistance from her gave her the gentlest of kisses.

Her lips demanded more and Leslie did not hesitate to counter with an urgency that defied all his breeding and moral concepts. This woman made him feel important and in more ways than simply being a good father to her child. He felt loved and needed by a beautiful and desirable woman. It had been such a long time.

They could not wait to get back to his room at the hotel. They had already indulged themselves with fine wine and a delicious cuisine at one of Paris's finest. Now, the desert that was nowhere to be found on the menu was about to be shared the piece de resistance.

***

They awoke together the next morning sharing a smile as well. Both felt fulfilled with their individual fantasies having been completed.

Sex was very good with Jason, but this was more exciting. Naturally, the thrill of being with another man was part of it, but it was more than that. This was the type of man she had dreamed about and now he was laying beside her in all his manhood.

Leslie was just as intoxicated with Amy. The sex had never been that great with Maggie because her heart was never into it. She only did it for the sexual need that all animals desire. He wondered if it was like this between Maggie and Jonathan's father when they had been together those two weeks.

He did not want to think about that anymore.

"Was this a mistake, Leslie?"

"Not at all, Amy. It had to happen. It just feels right. I love Maggie, but she doesn't give me what I need from a woman. Simply put, you do." He reached over and kissed her lips softly.

"It is somewhat different for me, Leslie. Jason does give me what I need and expect from a man, but I will be open with you and share my guilty pleasure...I have always desired a man of class...a man like you."

"Is it what you expected?"

"More," she responded as she returned his kiss. "Do we have time for more desert?" she laughed.

He grabbed her and they wrestled across the bed and then like the end of a storm they cuddled back into oblivion.

Chapter 28*Christmas

Jason had wanted kids and shared that desire with Amy from the start. However, she was more interested in helping her dad build the business and enjoying life with her new husband and new lover for that matter.

For that reason she had abstained from intercourse with Jason during ovulation and would always come up with a good reason. Before marriage she submitted to him at will and he used proper protection.

However, when in Paris in November she was ovulating and indeed very fertile. Not to her surprise she missed her time of the month shortly thereafter.

She had begun to worry about it as soon as she started for home in late November. Now, it has become a reality and she has no idea what to do about it. Fortunately, she had sex with Jason in November as well before going to France. Therefore, if she is pregnant Jason will believe it is his child. Most likely, however, it is Leslie's child, but she would not know for certain.

***

It was two days before Christmas and she left the doctor's office wondering if she could hide her worst fear when telling Jason that she is pregnant. She would wait until Christmas Eve and make an announcement to the whole family which would include Jason's parents and her parents.

She would not tell Leslie that it was his. She was not positive anyway.

***

Christmas Eve was spent at the mansion in Highland Park. Robert and Elizabeth had invited Jason's parents, John and Susan, making it a fully extended family affair.

The home was decorated to the extreme. Money was no object. Tables were lined with hors d'oeuvres, the bar was open and gifts lined the bottom of the seven foot tree which was flown in from Oregon.

John and Susan had not been in the Van Horn home even though their kids went together for over twelve years, actually eight when you exclude the four years of war.

143

The senior Alexanders were not poor people by any means, but this kind of opulence was far above their station in life. They looked forward to being out among the wealthy for a change. They were so thankful to Robert for giving their son the opportunity to make a good life for himself and his wife.

Robert fixed drinks for everyone having let the staff off for the night to enjoy their own Christmas. The group got along quite well and bonds were forming to the delight of Jason and Amy.

A little business was discussed and then Elizabeth told Robert to forget about business for tonight and enjoy Christmas. She was soft spoken, but when she did make a demand Robert took heed. She was the strong, silent woman behind the prosperousbusiness man. He had always respected her for her influence.

It was time to open presents. Jason was about to become Santa when Amy stood and asked everyone to give her their attention.

"I have a special gift for all of you," she began. "I am carrying Jason's child."

"What?" shouted Jason.

"Halleluiah", Robert chimed in and reached over to shake John's hand.

The two grandmothers looked proudly at one another and smiled.

Jason took Amy into his arms and gave her a big squeeze.

"I'm going to be a father?"

"Yes," she answered as she smiled up at him..

It would be a terrific Christmas.

Chapter 29*Pretense

It was a cold evening in February, 1948 and Amy was showing just enough that it was easily camouflaged with her current collection of dresses and suits. She had plans to see Leslie while in London and did not want him to know she was pregnant just yet. She would tell him on her next trip. Of course, he would be able to tell by then anyway.

***

They met at her hotel and shared drinks at the bar. She could not wait to take him upstairs and make love. After all, she was almost positive this child was his, so she was not being a horrible person.

Okay, she thought to herself, *I know I am a horrible person either way, but this just seems so right for some reason. I just know this is Leslie's child and I want to continue our sexual relationship. I love these two men in different ways.*

They arrived at her room and Leslie could barely prevent himself from tearing at her clothes before the door to the room was fully closed. She reached for the light not wanting him to see her tummy just yet.

Maybe next time.

***

Jason was in Paris and Maggie was in class in Torrance. Amy and Leslie only had to be careful when in their working environments where people knew them both and rumors could fly.

They tried to be very professional when together and it was fairly often since Harvey Wickham department stores were partial to Van Horn designs that were more accommodating to their demographic customer.

***

Maggie was a very good teacher because she loved her work and adored the kids. She watched the first and second graders from afar and looked forward to them coming into her third grade class.

Jonathan was just two months shy of his second birthday and because he was born in April would have to wait until September of 1953 to begin first grade.

That's okay, she thought. *Better than being younger than most.*

He would be entering school under the name of Jonathan Chapman, a fine British name indeed, but Maggie knew his name should be Jonathan Alexander, a proud American name.

***

Leslie was a good father figure to Jonathan. He was always holding him and cutting up with him and bringing home toys that the two of them enjoyed together.

He was proud to call him a Chapman, but often wondered what his name would have been. Maggie would never talk about the birth father.

Leslie would continue to raise him as his own and provide for his mother. Unfortunately, he was in over his head with this other woman and was beating himself up about it. He could not convince himself that Maggie deserved this dishonesty.

Amy had a stranglehold on him and the two of them were caught up in the pretense of being faithful spouses. He wished it were not so.

***

Leslie arrived home late to find supper still on the table. He was late and that was not normal behavior for him. He worked hard, but when he was in England he always arrived home in time for supper.

Maggie was not upset as was her manner. She understood his duties were very demanding and expected this would happen on occasion.

They hugged and he gave her a kiss as Jonathan tugged at his pants leg. Leslie reached down and picked him up as he normally did and as Jonathan had begun to expect. Leslie's world was back to normal.

Chapter 30*Explanation

It was June of 1948 and time for Jason to return to London. This time, he would need to stay an extended period of time due to some managerial problems. He realized that Maggie would be out of school and Leslie would most likely be out of the country. This may well be a time that he and Maggie can see each other without interference from their spouses.

He felt that he needed time with her to fully explain what happened when he sailed home from France. She deserved a more definitive answer to an insoluble situation.

He called Leslie's office and asked his secretary if he could speak with him. She told him that Mr. Chapman was out of the office. Jason told her who he was and caught her attention immediately. He asked if Leslie would be in the next day. The secretary explained that Mr. Chapman was out of the country on business and would not return for one week. Jason felt a rush of blood flow to his chest. This was his chance.

He thanked the secretary and told her that he would catch him next visit.

Jason went to Van Horn London to take care of some business knowing full well that his heart would not be in it. He was thinking only of Maggie.

He met with Mr. Quimby, the Van Horn London store manager. Quimby, as he preferred to be called was a Brit with a vast knowledge of fashion, but very little understanding of people and their needs as employees.

Jason had been informed of problems with store personnel through the grapevine. All he was told was that Quimby was hard to work for and employees were disgruntled. Jason realized that he needed to spend some quality time at the store and deal with the situation.

"How are you doing, Quimby?" Jason asked politely.

"Jolly good, sir," the elderly gentleman replied. "And you, sir?"

"I am doing quite well. Thank you for asking Quimby. So Quimby, how do you get along with the staff?"

"Well, sir, we have our problems, but that must exist in most business situations," he replied with a strong British accent.

"Would you be offended if I were to talk to each employee individually?" asked Jason as if to give Quimby control of the issue.

"Not at all sir. After all, you are my superior."

Jason thanked him and shook his hand, then walked toward the back of the store to where most of the employees would be found.

The employees all recognized Jason by now and felt really comfortable in his presence. They had a feeling as to why he was here this time. Word spread that unhappy employees had let it be known of their current state of affairs.

Jason singled out a young lady that walked the runway. She was tall, thin and beautiful in appearance, but not the kind of beauty that captured Jason's attention. Maggie was still his image of what beauty should be.

"Hello, Sonja," Jason called out as the girl with legs up to her neck came toward him.

"Well, hello, Jason. Jolly good to see you."

Jason had informed everyone in both stores to please call him by his first name. Naturally, Quimby simply referred to him as Sir.

"Will you join me in Quimby's office?" Jason politely asked.

She followed Jason further back past the dressing rooms to a small, unassuming office that was cluttered with designs.

"Okay, Sonja, tell me what seems to be the problem with Quimby and the staff."

"Well, he is just so set in his ways. He is old school I guess and simply does not understand how to treat us younger lassies and lads. He probably is a nice old gent, but he evidently has no background that included interacting with people.

"Blimey, he can be so rude," she said with a show of emotion.

"Now, I must give him this," she continued. "He never comes back to the dressing rooms. He isn't a dirty old man, if you know what I mean. And, he really knows fashion. He knows what

153

sells and he knows what doesn't sell, but he leaves the modeling to us gals and the attendants in the dressing rooms."

"So, it all boils down to personalities and respect for others?" Jason concluded.

"That's correct, sir," she answered using the polite address to show her respect for Jason's attention to her grievances.

Jason did not need to talk to others. This was a simple case of age differences and personality conflicts. He would talk with Quimby in private.

"Quimby, I have to leave now, but would like to have lunch with you tomorrow."

"That would be most pleasant, sir."

Jason left for his hotel and the phone that would be there. He was so anxious to hear her voice.

***

"Hello"

"Hi Maggie."

"Jason!"

154

"Yes, Maggie. It's me. Can you talk?"

"Oh, yes, just me and Jonathan. I am out for the summer and no need for my mum to keep him. I want to be with him as much as possible during the summer."

"That's great, Maggie. I bet he is a handsome little man."

She paused thinking how much she thought Jonathan looked like his dad.

"Yes, he is, just like his daddy," she smiled knowing that she had just shared something with Jason without his realizing the true intention.

"Maggie, I am in town for a week and I know from calling Leslie's office that he will be gone for a week. I need to see you. Please say, 'yes'."

"I want to see you as well, Jason. If you take a taxi it should be safe for us to be at my home. My parents will not come over unannounced and you won't have a car in front of my home to draw attention. Does that sound okay?"

"That is perfect. That gives me a chance to see your son as well. I will be there around dark just for a little more precaution."

***

The taxi drive seemed to take forever even though it was only an hour. Jason was so anxious. He squirmed in his seat anticipating what he would say.

He arrived as the sun went down. It was a quiet neighborhood and the houses were not all that close together. Like Maggie's, each home sat on an acre or two of land allowing more privacy than in most communities. This would be fine.

He knocked on the door and Maggie opened it. Jason was so enamored by her appearance that he almost did not see the little boy standing beside his mommy.

"Come in, Jason."

Jason entered and shook hands as if they were strangers.

"Mommy, who is that man?" asked the little boy clinging to his mother.

Oh, how she wished she could tell him.

"This is a friend of your daddy's," she answered unwillingly. "His name is Mr. Alexander."

"My, what a great looking kid Maggie!"

"Thank you, Jason," she smiled sympathetically.

"How old is he?"

Maggie hesitated and then replied, "He just turned two," she lied. *That would make it eleven months after Jason left Europe,* she thought to herself.

Jonathan was actually two years and two months.

"Wow! He is big for his age," Jason exclaimed.

Maggie just agreed.

"I have fixed us something to eat. If you are hungry we can eat now before I put Jonathan to bed," Maggie quickly suggested.

"Starved," answered Jason.

They moved to the dining room table and enjoyed a quiet meal as Jonathan played with his food. They shared some laughs and caught up on current events in both of their lives as Maggie thought to herself how this setting is the way it is supposed to be.

After dinner, Maggie had Jonathan say goodnight to Jason and then put him to bed for the night.

She returned to Jason who was now sitting on the same sofa he enjoyed almost three years ago. There was one difference, however. The photo on the table beside him was no longer of Leslie, but instead of Leslie and Maggie.

Maggie sat down beside him but not too close. She desperately wanted to.

"Maggie, I have never let you out of my mind. The love we had was immeasurable. I wanted so badly to hold on to what we found here three years ago, but all the variables that engulfed me back home were immensely supportive of letting go and doing the right thing by Amy and our families.

"It has eaten away at my heart ever since. After three years I still look at you and know deep down that I truly love you in a way I could never love another."

Maggie reached out her hand and laid it on top of his. There was a moment of silence as they stared into each other's eyes.

"I have never stopped loving you, either, Jason. It breaks my heart every time I see you and I can't touch you or have you hold me the way I dream about at night. I have a son and husband to consider now. I can not let my feelings for you destroy the life we have planned for Jonathan."

"I understand, Maggie. I know you are right and you must put your son first. We are expecting our first child as well and I am sure things will change for me when I first hold that infant in my arms."

"Oh Jason, I am so happy for you both!"

She really meant that, but at the same time it hurt to know another woman was carrying Jason's child.

However, that was yet to be known. Was it Jason's unborn child, or Leslie's?

"Maggie, may I put my arms around you? I just want to remember how it felt."

Maggie moved toward him as he wrapped his arms around her waist and she put her arms around his neck. They just sat there quietly embracing.

"Whose girl are you?"

"I'm your girl, Yank."

"And don't you forget it."

They both wanted so badly to kiss and make love, but each one had decided thatthey needed to be strong for their children and of course for their life partners.

***

Jason arrived at the pub where he and Quimby had decided beforehand to meet. It was just around the corner from Van Horn and according to Quimby served the finest ale and sandwiches in all of London.

They visited for a few moments while Quimby explained the menu to Jason. Jason eyed the cute waitress as he listened. She seemed to know everyone there.

"Hello, guv'nor," she greeted Quimby in her cockney accent. Quimby explained later that she was from the east end of London, thus the accent.

"Hello, Mary. How are you today?" greeted Quimby.

"Doing as well as can be expected with all these flirts in here. Just won't leave their mitts off me, they won't."

"Well, you just come and see old Quimby next one that bothers you, Lassie."

"Thank you, guv'nor. What would you two gentlemen like to order?"

"Bring us a couple of ales for now and we will decide on lunch in a bit."

She wiggled off as Quimby's eyes followed.

"Quimby, you seem to have a way with the ladies. Why can't you be as pleasant with your staff?"

"Well, Sir, I believe there should be a line between in the shop and outside the shop. I don't want them to be my friends at Van Horn. I want them to respect me and do their jobs," he answered politely.

"Quimby, you can be a friend to someone and still gain their respect as an employer or manager. The girls in the shop say you are almost mean to them and they have very little respect for you. It is very important to keep your staff happy in their jobs. Once they become disgruntled it is only a matter of time before it reflects on their performance to their duties.

"Why not pick a happy medium between the way you respond to them and the way I just saw you respond to Mary? I believe you will find a common ground that will make all concerned happy and fulfilled in their jobs."

"I will work on it, Sir. I surely will and thank you for being so blunt. I respect that in a man. "Now, let me order you the finest sandwich in town," Quimby said as he snapped his fingers for Mary.

Chapter 31*Stella

It was June 1948 and Amy was seven months into her pregnancy. She and Leslie had made plans to meet in Paris while their spouses were in London and Torrance respectively.

Amy anticipated trouble from Leslie at the sight of her belly. She had invited him up to her room overlooking the Seine where memories of their first sexual encounter would possibly stir his desires rather than let the impact of her pregnancy bring about another reaction entirely.

She did not want him making a scene in the hallway, so she left the door ajar and yelled to him to enter when he knocked.

She was standing in front of the window looking out over the river as he entered.

"Oh, my God is it good to see you!" he exclaimed as he rushed to her.

She turned around and he just froze in his tracks.

"Amy, I thought you didn't want children?" he blurted out in dismay.

"I didn't, but I was careless as you can see."

"How many months along are you?"

"Seven," she smiled.

You could see him doing the quick math...

"It's mine?"

"I am sure it is, but we can't be certain because I slept with Jason in November as well."

She explained her avoidances with Jason and her fertility with him that last time together here in Paris.

"So, I am almost certain that you are the father, but we can not let it be known for everyone's sake."

Leslie sighed, "You and Jason raising my child! I don't know how we can handle that."

Well, Maggie and I are doing the same thing with Jonathan and have handled it just fine, he thought to himself.

"Come here, baby. I need you," Amy requested in a sulky voice.

"Are you sure it is okay?"

"It will be just fine," she grinned.

***

It was a hot August morning as Jason rushed Amy to the Easton General Hospital. He had called ahead and they were ready for her. The Van Horns always received special attention.

She was holding Jason's hand as two men in white carted her into the delivery room.

"You will have to remain here," one of the men told Jason.

"I love you," Jason said for the first time realizing that she was about to give him a child and, that surely would draw them closer together, especially him.

She was in too much pain to respond.

The Van Horns and the John Alexanders were all there anxious to see their new grandchild and eager to hear whether it was a boy or girl. The doctor came out and asked who the father was.

"I am," replied Jason as he rose to the occasion. "Is she okay?"

"Your wife and baby are both doing just fine. You have a healthy baby girl," smiled the doctor.

"Thank you, doctor," Jason grinned as he gave him a bear hug.

There were hugs all around and relief on all their faces.

***

They all stood in front of the glass partition viewing the beautiful baby girl that had just come into the world. The four grandparents were googooing and wooing through the glass and acting silly like grandparents will do.

"Isn't she just beautiful," said Elizabeth.

"Wonder where she got that curly black hair?"

Leslie had black hair while Jason's hair was auburn.

"My mother had black hair," answered Susan proudly.

"I'm just glad she is healthy," responded Jason. "When will they let me see her?"

"As soon as Amy awakes, they will take the baby to her and you will probably be allowed in the room at that time," replied his mom.

***

They finally told Jason to go in and he jumped up eager to see his daughter. He went into the room where Amy had just finished nursing and noticed a great big smile on Amy's face. He was so glad to see that response since she had not seemed eager to have kids.

"Hi sweetie. How are you feeling?" he asked inquisitively.

"We are both doing just fine, honey. Say hello to Stella."

They had both decided on names whichever way it went. This name came from a popular song, Stella by Starlight.

"Pick her up," Amy told the new father.

"Are you sure?"

"Go ahead, silly. There is nothing to it," she giggled.

He stood there holding his child and just like the grandparents before him, started googooing and wooing. Amy got a good laugh from watching and a warm and fuzzy feeling in her stomach, but then her memory turned to Leslie who was probably the real father. *Oh, God. Please let Stella be Jason's daughter and if not, please don't let him know about the real father.*

Chapter 32*Absence

There would be a period of time when Jason and Maggie would not see each other, nor would Amy and Leslie for that matter since Amy would take another couple of months off from work.

Jason had resigned himself to the fact that he and Maggie were a thing of the past while Amy was slowly getting attached to her baby girl. Motherhood seemed to take her mind off of Leslie and more toward the man that would be raising her child.

Jason's natural child was across the sea and Jason was not aware. Leslie's natural child could possibly be overseas as well and he was well aware.

Both Maggie and Amy were living in fear of discovery.

***

It was November 1948. Stella was almost three months and Amy was ready to return to work.

Jason had gone back to Europe a month earlier. They both needed to do a lot of catching up.

Amy was already thinking ahead to seeing Leslie again. She was consumed with leading this double life, especially now when she believed Leslie was the father of her child and Jason was still her husband. She wanted them both in her life.

Back she went to London and booked a room with a view of the Thames River. She would do some sight seeing this time even though it was chilly this time of year.

She would visit a pub and enjoy ale on the east side and she would visit a fancy restaurant in central London and have an upscale dinner.

Then, on to some of the castles in the region, something she had always wanted to do. She just wished she was sharing this adventure with one of her two men who were both in Paris.

Maybe she would call up Maggie to join her on the weekend who could show her some of the other legendary attractions. *Why not?*

Maggie was very receptive to Amy's invitation. She would join her on Saturday while Jonathan visited his grandparents. She wanted to feel the presence of Jason any way she could and this was the only outlet she had at this time besides raising his child.

Amy took care of business the following day which was on a Friday and then left for the day with Maggie that Saturday morning after joining her for breakfast in the hotel restaurant.

She decided to let Maggie pick the places to visit since she had lived here her entire life. Maggie would be her tour guide.

***

They visited the National Gallery in Trafalgar Square with Western European paintings from the thirteenth to nineteenth centuries by such artists as Van Gogh and Renoir, the Natural History Museum with its dinosaur collection, Somerset House with impressionist and post-impressionist paintings, the Tower of London and of course Buckingham Palace.

What a great day they were having and they were becoming such good friends.

Maggie could never know about her and Leslie, Amy thought.

Amy could never know about her and Jason, Maggie thought.

***

170

Leslie walked into Van Horn Paris not expecting to see Jason. He assumed Jason and Amy would stay home awhile longer with *his* new baby.

He spotted Jason as soon as he entered the store with Pierre going over the garments that had just arrived from New York.

Leslie would take care of some buying and then hopefully have lunch with Jason and listen to him talk about *his* baby. Leslie wanted all the details. He may never see hisdaughter. At least, there was a pipeline to his child through Jason or Amy.

Leslie did find many ladies apparel that he knew would sell back home and with the help of Pierre placed a rather large order.

He approached Jason and asked if he would care to join him for lunch. Jason agreed as he was anxious to tell his friend all about *his* daughter.

They ventured down to the tourist area and found a small restaurant that was know for its pastries. Jason had a sweet tooth.

Inside was a bustling crowd of young people from the garment industry and banking industry that congregated there often.

All the talk was of fashion and marketing and of course banking. Leslie and Jason enjoyed being in the midst of all the gaiety and laughter. Neither had spent much time with other men lately. They were both consumed with their respective jobs and their new families.

"So, tell me about Stella," Leslie began.

"You must have seen Amy on her last trip to Paris?" Jason questioned.

"Yes, she caught me by surprise when I walked into Van Horn and there she was out to here," he demonstrated with his hands.

"Was it expected?"

"Not at all," responded Jason. "We had not planned it. We were both too busy. Just one of those things."

"Tell me about her," Leslie anxiously asked.

"Well, she is average size with black curly hair and smiles all the time like her mom. She sleeps pretty well through the night, so it hasn't been too hard on us. She must get that from me. I am a sound sleeper."

I am a sound sleeper as well. She gets that from me, Leslie thought to himself. *And the black hair,* he mused.

"Is she as pretty as her mom?"

"Definitely," answered Jason, "And she looks like she may turn out to be tall with those long legs of hers," he grinned.

Of course she will, Leslie thought. *I have long legs.*

"How is your son doing?" Jason asked showing interest in Leslie's family.

"Oh my, the lad is growing like a weed and is just as jolly a lad as there could possibly be," responded Leslie appreciatively. "Thank you for asking."

"And Maggie, how is she doing coping with teaching and raising a child?"

"She is doing very well, Jason. She is simply a wonderful woman and a great mom."

"How about great wife?" Jason countered. "Sorry, that is none of my business."

"Quite alright, my good fellow. You and I are becoming good friends and are bonded together in business. I think men in those situations do tell one another personal things. We live in a more modern society today.

"To answer your question, I am not a very happy man. My wife still loves another man. I probably should not be telling you that, but I need to share with someone."

Jason's heart beat rapidly. He knew Maggie loved him, but hearing it from her husband made it all that more solidified. It was so sad to hear. On one side, a man who does not feel love from his wife and on the other side, a man who still loves that woman under discussion. A sad, sad state of affairs, indeed.

"I stay with her because I love her deeply and because we have a son together and because I continue to hope that she will grow to love me."

"Very admirable of you, Leslie. A lesser man would walk out if he knew for sure that his wife did not love him, or even worse loved another man."

"Well, I went in with my eyes wide open. She told me upfront that she loved me, but was not in love with me. I guess there is a difference?" Leslie gestured with his hands up in the air.

"Well, Leslie…like I said, it takes an admirable man to stand by your woman."

Oh, how I long for Maggie, Jason reflected.

Oh, how I yearn for this man's wife right now, dreamed Leslie. *She bore my child. I have every right.*

Chapter 33 *New York

It was December, 1949. Amy had been with Leslie a couple of times over the past year, once in Paris and again in London. She would work it out so that Jason was either home with Stella or was at the opposing city from where she was working.

Both Leslie and Amy were becoming comfortable with their arrangement and feeling less guilty because of their commonly shared baby girl. At least they were ninety-nine percent sure of that anyway.

***

This would be Stella's second Christmas, but the first one where she was old enough to actually appreciate her toys.

The whole family was there again surrounded by food and drink at the lavish home of the Van Horns.

Naturally, they all overdid the gift bearing, so many gifts for such a tiny child. She would look at one and immediately set it aside in order to go after the next one.

Amy and Jason were pretending to have the perfect marriage and family and in some respects they actually were. They rarely had a fight. They both adored Stella and each one took a large part in caring for her when they were home.

In the same token, Maggie and Leslie were also giving a good performance in their marriage. They, like the Alexanders were crazy about Jonathan, and their family life seemed almost perfect to the observing eye.

Deep down, Maggie longed for Jason's touch and Jason felt the same innermost feelings for her. Despite their longing for each other they went on with their lives giving all they had to making the most of what they felt was the best choice for their children.

***

The shutdown of Manhattan over various strikes had been over for a couple of years now and the fashion industry was playing catch up to Europe's post-war thrust into the market.

Van Horn started emerging once again in New York as the premiere marketer of women's apparel in the low to middle income bracket. When at home, both Amy and Jason would work the metropolitan area. Life was very busy for this working mom and dad.

***

Florence, Italy would burst onto the scene in the fifties which would spread Jason, Leslie and Amy even thinner. There were now four major fashion capitals in London, Paris, Florence and New York.

Van Horn Fashions was doing extremely well and Robert gave much of the reward to his daughter and son-in-law.

Leslie would now come to New York to buy from the various designers. This would give him and Amy more opportunities to be together. They were spinning a web that could very easily trap them both.

***

It was 1952 and the Korean War was in full motion. Leslie had flat feet and therefore was not accepted in the British services during World War II and now would miss the Korean.

As for Jason, he was on disability and would not be called up again. He felt like the disability label was unnecessary since he was living a very normal life, but the army thought

otherwise. He still had not redeemed any memories from his past.

***

Leslie was in Manhattan and called Amy at their new

home in Summers Landing knowing full well from a previous

encounter with Amy that Jason would be out of the country. She

agreed to meet him at his hotel where they would make love prior to

going out for dinner and wine.

***

They left the hotel after showering and headed for Long

Island where no one should recognize Amy even though she did

have an account there. The chances were very slim.

***

Leslie wanted to see his daughter. He felt like this was

the perfect opportunity now that he was adding New York to his

business travels. Amy was eager for that as well, but was concerned

about repercussions.

They both decided to take the chance.

***

It was on a Saturday morning that Amy drove with her daughter to meet the man whom she thought was Stella's natural father. Again, they would meet in Long Island, but this time in a park.

Leslie was already there anxiously awaiting the arrival of his daughter. Amy parked and took Stella from the car and walked slowly with the toddler toward him.

With a smile that spread across his entire face Leslie reached down and picked Stella up and just stared at her. Amy felt compassion for him knowing what it must mean to see your child for the very first time. Stella was nearing four years of age.

They had a grand time playing on the swings and slide, laughing and chasing Stella around the park. It was a beautiful thing to see from Amy's viewpoint. She felt comfortable with her situation and believed she could continue to live in two worlds. Leslie would continue to see Stella as often as possible and she would begin to know him as Uncle Leslie.

Chapter 34*First Grade

It was September of 1953. Jonathan had turned six in April of the previous year. Maggie could now start taking him to school with her and give the grandparents a break from babysitting. After all, her parents were in their early fifties and still had a life of their own.

Jonathan was excited at attending the first day of school as was Leslie who had arranged to be in town for this special life event.

The two parents proudly walked hand in hand with Jonathan as they entered the building and took him to his first grade class.

They entered the classroom and Leslie was introduced by Maggie to Jonathan's teacher. They watched as Jonathan was shown to his chair and he waved goodbye as they left through the doorway with tears in their eyes.

At least mom would always be close by.

Maggie was beginning to notice certain characteristics in Jonathan that were very similar to Jason. She wondered if Leslie had noticed those similarities as well.

Oh, how she longed for Jason. The years were flying by and still she thought of him and wanted him in her life.

Impossible, she thought. *I can't let Jason know. It would make him want to be with us and I just can not have that kind of disruption in Jonathan's life.*

***

The years went by quickly and Jonathan was entering the third grade. Now, his mom would also be his teacher.

On several occasions Jonathan called out, "Mum," instead of Mrs. Chapman as his mom had stressed to him. All the kids would giggle.

He was a very attentive and good student and made all A's. Of course, the other kids called him teacher's pet, but deep down they knew that living with the teacher there was no way Jonathan was going to get out of doing his homework.

Leslie would drop in on the class whenever possible and let Jonathan know that he was interested in his school work.

Jonathan was all smiles when his dad and mom were both in the classroom.

Chapter 35*Coincidence

Jason was needed back in London. It was a warm sunny day and he had left Van Horn London for a bite to eat when he noticed someone across the street from him that looked very familiar. It was a woman and a young boy.

As they drew nearer and were directly across from him, he realized suddenly that it was Maggie and probably her son. His heart skipped a beat as he started toward her only to be honked at as he stepped in front of an oncoming motorist. It provided a memory of his and Maggie's first meeting.

He reached the other side of the street and called out to her. The woman turned and her face went white as though she had seen a ghost.

Jason hurried toward her and reached out his hand. She extended hers and they smiled warmly at each other as their hands clutched in a stronger than normal handshake.

Wow, does she look wonderful, he thought. It had been eight years if memory served and she was more beautiful than ever.

Oh, if only her child wasn't here, I would take her into my arms, he imagined.

"Hello, Jason," offered Maggie. "It has been a long time."

"Yes, it has Maggie. Eight years, in fact. I believe I have counted every day," he countered without being ashamed.

"I know, Jason. It has been a very long time indeed."

"Mum, why has he counted the days?" asked the young boy.

"Oh, some people have habits of keeping up with time and Mr. Alexander is one that does that. He is very good at it, Jonathan.

"Do you remember Mr. Alexander?"

"No, ma'am."

"Well, you were only two the last time you saw him, honey. He is a business friend of your dad's."

"Hello, Jonathan. I assumed that it was you. You must be ten years old now."

"Yes, sir," he answered proudly.

185

Maggie stood there admiring the way the two were communicating. She wished so much that the three of them were together and out for the day on a getaway, mom, dad and son, Jason's son. She was tormented by her feelings.

"Maggie, can we have lunch? My treat," Jason smiled at the eager young man who was feeling his first hunger pang.

"Why not?" responded Maggie. "Is that okay with you, son?"

"I want a hamburger, mum."

"Jonathan, that isn't very good manners. Let Mr. Alexander decide where we go," Maggie scolded light heartedly.

"Hamburger, it is," Jason gleefully responded. "Where can we get one like they make in the U.S.?"

"As a matter of fact, they have opened a place close by that serves American burgers and malts. It's called Yank Burgers," she laughed reminding Jason of the time she called him a Yank.

"Great!" shouted out Jason as he winked at Jonathan and off they went.

"My goodness," exclaimed Maggie. "That is the best burger ever!"

"Me too," agreed Jonathan with a mouth full of food.

"Don't talk with your mouth full, Jonathan."

She looked at Jason across the table and gave him a look that he knew very well. He felt the same way. He wanted her so badly. It was tearing him apart to continue living a lie.

They left the establishment and both had so much they wanted to say, but knew they could not. They continued to express their longing for each other through their eyes.

Maggie said her goodbyes and gave him a slight hug. Jason reached down and started to hug Jonathan, but suddenly stopped and said, "Wait a moment. You are too big for a hug. Give me a handshake, young man."

Jonathan stood tall and grinned as they shook hands. If only Jason knew...

Chapter 36*JFK

November 22, 1963, a date that remains with most Americans and many people worldwide as the day America changed forever.

Jason and Amy were arriving at Idlewild Airport coming home together from a trip to Milan, the newest fashion capital on the world scene.

The trip was very successful and they were both exhausted and eager to get home to their daughter and the peace and relaxation of their den.

They heard the news in the lobby of the airport and like everyone else were in total disbelief. They hurried home to be with their daughter when she got home from school. They knew she would have questions. She was a freshman in their old high school and becoming a very popular teen.

Jonathan was a junior at his local high school and like most Brits was really taken aback by the assassination news. He felt the urge to do something, but didn't know what that would be. He was becoming a very cultivated young man with adventure growing in his veins. He felt there was something more to his life than playing soccer and dating the local girls.

Maggie and Leslie were shocked as well by the news. Maggie knew full well how devastated Jason must be. She wished she could be there for him.

Leslie was in New York and felt the hurt that surrounded him everywhere. It was a sad day in the states. He also wished he could be with Amy and comfort her.

It would be quite awhile before that sad day in Dallas would not be the main topic of every conversation.

The Italians were making an impact on the fashion world and Van Horn needed to get back to work and get their minds off the shooting.

Chapter 37*Vacation

The summer of 1965 would prove to be an eventful and emotional time for both the Chapman family and the Alexander family.

Jason and Leslie had continually run into each other over the years and their friendship had grown into one of mutual respect and admiration.

Jason saw an opportunity to take advantage of their friendship and spend time with the love of his life.

He had asked Leslie if he would be interested in a joint family vacation in the south of France sometime in July of 1965. Jason's supposed daughter Stella just finished her junior year in high school and Leslie's supposed son Jonathan had just finished his freshman year at Leslie and Maggie's alma mater, Cambridge.

Leslie, of course thought it a splendid idea. What a great way to spend time with his natural daughter and his lover.

***

Plans were booked and the two families arrived in Valence, a small village in the southeast of France sitting alongside the Rhone River.

Jonathan had grown into a very handsome man looking very much like his natural father, Jason, but not enough to make Leslie take notice.

Stella, while only one month shy of her seventeenth birthday and heading into her senior year in high school had matured into a lovely young woman acquiring many of her mother's genes.

Upon meeting the Chapman's son she grinned from ear to ear. *What a beautiful man!*

Her mom caught the look in her daughter's eye and cringed. *Oh, no you don't*, she said to herself. *I better keep an eye on this situation.*

Stella was only two years younger than Jonathan and he found her very attractive as well. Both Leslie and Amy noticed the attraction. However, it did not bother Leslie since he was aware that he was not the biological father of Jonathan. He had never shared that with Amy for Maggie's sake.

On the other hand, it was still possible that Stella was Jason's daughter and the half-sister of Jonathan. Of course, nobody realized that scenario except Maggie.

Both Maggie and Amy found themselves in a peculiar set of circumstances and neither wanted anything romantic to evolve from these two young people.

Meanwhile, it had been nine years since Jason and Maggie's last encounter. It was exactly twenty years since they first met and fell in love. They took one hard look at one another and realized the feelings were still instilled in the both of them.

They were both forty-five now and still very attractive and physically fit. They made every effort to not stare at one another, but found themselves doing so more than once during that first gathering of their respective families.

Leslie and Amy had been together so many times by now that it was much easier for them to play their proper roles as devoted spouses. They just hoped they would find an opportunity to have some private time together.

They all had already checked into their rooms and were greeting one another in the hotel lobby. Everyone was hungry and agreed to try the patio overlooking the Rhone. It was July, but a cool breeze was coming in off the river. It would be very refreshing to sit outside and share in a drink before dinner.

The conversations were mostly about business between the parents while the two teens were talking of their schools and what it was like growing up in England versus the United States.

Stella was intrigued by this very mature young man and his desires to achieve something special in his life.

Jonathan, on the other hand was fascinated by her intellect and beauty. The two were being scrutinized carefully by their moms.

***

The next day, they all went to the museum within walking distance and immersed themselves in the history of this quaint town and its Armenian heritage.

As they wandered aimlessly through the adjoining rooms, Maggie found herself lagging behind. Jason noticed and slowed down as the others ventured on.

He reversed his field and returned to Maggie where she was involved in a work of art. He walked up behind her and gently placed his hands on her waist.

"Whose girl are you," he spoke softly.

Without turning around she said,

"I'm your girl, Yank."

"And don't you forget it," as he repeated those same words from twenty years before.

Maggie turned suddenly to catch his eyes staring down toward hers and they had this sudden desire to kiss. It had been twenty years since they last kissed and this was the perfect opportunity amongst the Armenian culture.

Their lips touched and it was as if they had never been apart. The magic was still there. The kiss lasted for what seemed several minutes, but actually was just for a moment, but that moment was frozen in time.

They knew they had to catch up with the others before someone noticed. They looked at each other and read into one another's eyes what their hearts were feeling.

***

They all walked along the river and watched as the local fishermen sat on the bank with their kids sitting beside them.

It seemed like a very normal day among friends. Only the good Lord knew for sure just how these friends connected in a family way.

***

That evening, they went to a local restaurant and tasted some French cuisine that was different from that in Paris due to its Armenian influence. They laughed and told stories and the kids were growing closer by the hour.

Throughout the week they relaxed on the bank of the Rhone, sat on the veranda and enjoyed meals together, rode into the hills in a sight seeing bus and wandered through the village shops. The week went extremely well and ended before each wanted it to end.

Chapter 38*Fun Times

Jonathan was back on campus starting his senior year. His major was English like his mom before him with a minor in social studies.

He was an excellent student and well respected by teachers and friends alike. He was always joining clubs and participating in causes.

The war in Vietnam was building rapidly and he wondered why Great Britain had not taken a stance as the United States had. The war began in 1950 with American advisors taking a small part in the fifties and strongly participating by 1961.

In 1965 the U.S. had active troops on the ground. Jonathan kept up with as much news as he could.

By his senior year in 1967 the war had escalated with thousands of American casualties. He felt strongly about helping his friends who had been his country's allies in two previous wars.

He took a stance to help in the fight, against a majority of youth who filled the campus grounds protesting the war. This was something he felt strongly about and he did not know how he could participate.

Jonathan wanted to spend spring break in New York with the Alexanders if he could get his parents to agree and fund the trip. He needed to be with those that were experiencing the tragedies of war first and second hand.

Mom and dad agreed to his trip knowing his adventurous nature needed to be nurtured. Mom was proud that he felt so strongly about troubles of others and was not a spoiled, self-centered young man like so many others.

***

He arrived at Kennedy International where Jason was waiting. Jason had talked to Leslie in London about Jonathan's wishes and was anxious to help in any way he could. He knew Amy would agree, at least that was his perception.

Of course, Amy could come up with no practical reason to deny such a visit, so the retreat was set. Stella was ecstatic!

Jason and Jonathan greeted one another graciously and this time unlike when Jonathan was ten, Jason gave him a big hug. He felt like an uncle to the young man.

They arrived in Summers Landing to a warm greeting at the front door by Stella who was watching impatiently from the front room for their arrival.

She hugged Jonathan and he noticed that she was even more beautiful two years later if such a thing were possible.

"You must be a sophomore at U Conn now," he remembered.

"Yes, and you are a senior Mr. Upperclassman, huh?" she kidded.

"That's right. Big man on campus," he returned the kidding.

"Honey, look who's here," explained Jason to Amy as they approached her in the kitchen where she was preparing lunch for everyone.

"Oh, my. Look at you. Such a fine looking young man," she said as she thought immediately how this was probably her daughter's half-brother. She had to feel something special for him for that reason alone.

"How proud your dad and mom must be," she finished with a hug around the neck.

"Thank you, ma'am. I hope they are."

"Let me show you your room."

Jonathan followed and Stella tagged along.

***

Jonathan wanted to see the sights of Manhattan and Stella was anxious to oblige. Amy did not know how to say no to her.

Off they went in Stella's Mustang heading for the train station. She was thrilled to be taking her British friend on an adventure. She knew Manhattan as well as her dad and just knew she could show Jonathan a good time.

The train ride was a thrill for the both of them. They felt like grownups as they sat in the diner car and had coffee.

Everything he said fascinated her. She found him to be so much more than the kids at U Conn. He had a magical presence about him and his personality was abundantly overwhelming to a young woman of almost twenty.

Jonathan would be turning twenty-two in August following graduation and was not sure of his plans quite yet. His future would probably include teaching, but there was something struggling within him that kept him up nights.

***

They arrived in Grand Central Station and it was everything Jonathan had heard about it. People were bustling everywhere like mice in a maze hurrying to their jobs or changing trains for other destinations.

Stella could not wait to show him the Empire State building, Times Square and especially to take him to see the Broadway play, 'I never sang for my father' on 48th street.

They went to the top of the Empire State building and he pretended to be Cary Grant pacing back and forth waiting for Deborah Kerr from the film, 'An Affair to Remember' which they both saw as teenagers.

200

Next, on to Times Square and all the excitement that goes with it. They spent at least two hours walking and gazing into windows.

She hoped tickets would be available for the play. With so many young men off to Vietnam there should not be a problem as business was slower than usual.

They were lucky and got fairly good seats for the popular play. They enjoyed it thoroughly.

The day had been a long one and she knew they needed to arrive home before midnight or she would hear about it from her dad. As long as she lived under his roof she would adhere to his rules.

They took the hour long ride back by train and talked all the way exchanging stories about their childhood and their high school days and of course the differences, if any in their campuses.

All in all, it was an outstanding day, one Stella would never forget. Jonathan was pleasantly surprised as well by how mature she was and how much fun they had together.

***

Jonathan wanted to talk as much as possible to Jason about his tour of duty in Europe. He wanted to know everything, but of course Jason could not tell him anything because he could not remember. Almost twenty-three years and he had not recovered a single memory.

Still, Jonathan wanted Jason to tell him what he could about Vietnam and what the men... actually boys, were going through over there. His parents did not like to discuss the horrors of war at home in England. They wanted to keep their son safe and hoped that England continued to choose not to get involved.

Jason informed him as much as he could, but that was only what he read or saw on television. He could be very little help to this inquisitive young man.

The rest of the week Jonathan and Stella drove around the countryside in Connecticut. He loved what he was seeing and would not mind staying longer, but school beckoned and he must get back

to England.

***

He said his goodbyes to the Alexanders and Stella drove

him to the train station. She had grown extremely fond of Jonathan

as he had with her, but they never took a step forward romantically

although Stella wanted to.

Jason had no way of knowing that his son was about to

take a dramatic leap of faith.

Chapter 39*Vietnam

Maggie and Leslie were so very proud of their son. He was about to graduate from Cambridge with honors and they just knew that he had a bright future ahead.

They gathered at the graduation ceremony with their parents who were now in their seventies. Both sets of grandparents had been very involved in Jonathan's life and he cared deeply for all of them.

Leslie's parents thought they were Jonathan's blood relatives just as Maggie's parents were. The secret had been maintained for Jonathan's entire life so far.

Jonathan had been seeing a girl on campus for the past year. It was nothing serious, but she joined the families for his graduation. The ten of them would all celebrate that evening and talk of Jonathan's life plans.

***

The party arrived at a London hot spot as the locals called it, the London Pad. Many of the graduates and their families and friends were already there and the drinks were pouring rapidly.

Jonathan had not been a partygoer for the most part preferring to spend quiet times with his girlfriend at a beach or restaurant or sharing time with friends with common interests.

Of course, he drank a few beers as did all the undergrads, but nothing stronger. Tonight would be the exception. It was bourbon and coke for Jonathan. He had noticed his Uncle Jason drinking that on their vacation together, so he thought he would give it a try.

Jack Daniel's black label and coke," he told the waiter.

His dad laughed aloud. "My son's first hard liquor," he announced.

The entire party shouted, "Jonathan's first whisky!"

"I once told Jason that was a college kid's drink jokingly, but he replied that he still loves it and bourbon and coke it shall remain."

The senior Chapmans and Maggie's parents were comfortable with tea. The night would end early for them.

Jonathan and his date, Tracy danced until their feet hurt and Jonathan was feeling no pain. Maggie asked him to slow down on the drinking.

"Sorry, Mum. I know I have had too much. I will be a good boy the rest of the night," he slurred his response.

Tracy was staying sober for the night and offered Jonathan some coffee.

The party soon ended and they all parted company. Tracy had her own car and said goodnight to Jonathan and his family.

***

Jonathan went into London to visit the army recruiting office. It was a small unattractive place with posters on the wall, two small desks and a couple of army sergeants sitting behind them.

"What can we do for you today young man?" asked the sergeant.

"I read something about how a Brit could go to Vietnam through a program called the Resignation/Re-enlistment Process," stated Jonathan.

"You read right. Is that what brought you here today?"

"Yes sir, I have a deep seeded desire to get involved because the Yanks were here for us in both world wars. I don't think it is right that we just sit back and let them and the Canadians do all the fighting."

The two sergeants looked at each other and smiled.

"What's your name, young man?"

"Jonathan, sir. Jonathan Chapman," he answered proudly.

"Well, Jonathan, that's a very proud statement and you make us proud. What all do you know about the program?"

"Well, sir, I know that I first would enlist in this man's army and then I would request a transfer to the army of the United States, or Canada. Then, I would be sent with their troops to Nam as one of their soldiers. Upon completion of my tour of duty I would resign from their army and re-enlist in the British army."

"That is exactly right," agreed the soldier.

"Are you ready to start the wheels in motion?"

"Yes, sir, I am, sir."

"All right then, let's get started filling out some papers."

Jonathan knew that telling his mom would be very difficult and she would try everything in her power to convince him to change his mind. He dreaded going home and facing her. He didn't think his dad would be as tough. He knew that his dad had tried to enlist and just maybe this would atone for his lack of duty for his country.

***

Maggie was in the back of the house. This was the same house she had rented over twenty-five years ago. She and Leslie purchased the home and put some money into it making it very comfortable for their needs. They were very happy here.

She greeted Jonathan as he approached her.

"Hi, Son. How was your day?"

"Mum, I have something to tell you."

She interrupted, "Don't tell me you're getting married," she laughed.

"No, Mum. This is serious."

She stopped what she was doing, lay the tool down that she used to plant her flowers and rose to look him straight into his eyes. She had never heard him sound so serious.

"What is it, Jonathan?" she asked frightened.

"Mum, you know how I am. I have always felt the need to reach out and extend a hand to my fellow man."

"Yes, son, I realize that."

"Well, I have been following the war in Vietnam throughout school and knew within that I needed to be there for our American friends."

Maggie covered her mouth with her hand.

"Mum, there is this program where I enlist in the British army, then transfer to the American army and go to Vietnam and when my tour of duty is done, I resign from the American army and re-enlist in our army. Well, I did that today."

"You did what today?" she shouted.

"I enlisted in the British army and filled out the forms for transfer to the American army."

"Oh, good Lord!" she exclaimed. "Oh, sweet Jesus!"

"Mum," he started, but she pulled away as he reached for her and ran into the house.

***

Leslie was working London that week and would be home for dinner. Maggie was waiting impatiently for him to get home. She had closed her door to her bedroom and was crying to herself. She did not want Jonathan to see her cry.

"I'm home!" yelled Leslie as was his custom. "Where is everyone?"

Jonathan was in his room and came out as soon as he heard his dad yell.

"Hey, Father, how are you?"

"I had a marvelous day, son. How about you?"

"I had a very momentous day, Father. I think you need to sit down."

"What is it? Where is your mother? Is she okay?" Leslie stumbled his words.

"She is in her room. I think she wants to be alone." Jonathan replied in a remorseful tone.

"Sit down, Father," he pointed to his father's favorite chair.

"Should I go get your mother first?"

"No, sir. She already knows what I am about to say to you."

Leslie looked bewildered as he sat comfortably in his recliner.

"Father, I joined the army today."

"You did what?" Leslie yelled as he came up out of his chair.

"Please sit down, sir. There is more," Jonathan said quite calmly.

Leslie sat back down in a non-committal position.

Jonathan began to explain the program he had embarked upon. His dad slowly committed to a sitting position in disbelief.

Jonathan finished and there was a silence. Then, Leslie asked how his mum was.

"I believe she is in her room crying."

"Let me go to her and we will all sit down and talk later," Leslie said in a low-keyed voice as he slowly walked toward his bedroom.

It was dinner time and no one had said a word. Leslie finally broke the silence asking for the salt.

"Mum, I understand how you feel. Believe me, I do. But I am twenty-two years old and still living at home with my parents. It is time for me to leave the nest and do what my heart tells me.

"I love you both with all my heart and realize the uncertainty that I face and the anguish both of you will share, but I truly believe this is my destiny. I want you both to wish me well and let me go without resentment."

His mom started crying again and Leslie put his arm around her.

"He is right, Maggie. It is his life and we must respect that."

Maggie looked up and looked at her son for the first time that night. "You have my blessing, son. God go with you," she cried.

Jonathan walked in the front door dressed in his army uniform. Leslie had gone to Milan and had wished him God speed before departing.

Maggie smiled and embraced her son and told him how handsome he looked in his uniform.

Jonathan told her that he would be leaving for America in less than a week for the new program.

They would spend as much time as possible together before his departure.

***

Maggie sat on the porch and pondered the situation she found herself in. She originally had declared along with Leslie that they would tell Jonathan who his biological father was on his eighteenth birthday. They had decided against that and only Maggie knew the reason why. She did not want to destroy Jason's family.

Now, however, their son was going off to war and the strong possibility existed that he may not come back. Jason would never forgive her if that happened and he later found out that Jonathan was his son.

213

She must tell Jonathan and Jason and at the same time let Leslie realize that the natural father was right there in front of him all along.

Chapter 40*His Son

Jonathan came into the breakfast room for his morning oatmeal and wheat toast. His mom seemed rather anxious as she placed the breakfast in front of him.

She thought she would let him enjoy his food before telling him.

He took his last sip of coffee and Maggie said,

"Jonathan, there is something I need you to know. You will probably hate me for not telling you sooner; much sooner, but I had my reasons. I hope you will someday appreciate those reasons."

Jonathan looked up with a puzzled expression on his face.

"Son, sometimes in life things happen that we don't plan on and we pay the consequences. But other times those mistakes produce wonderful results and that is what happened with me.

"I was almost as young as you at the close of the war and this young, handsome soldier from America came here on army orders for some relaxation.

"We met quite accidentally and spent some time together. We discovered that we really liked one another and decided to spend his entire two weeks in England together.

"We fell in love almost overnight. It was magical, son. I can't explain it any better than that. It grew leaps and bounds every day and night to the point where he did not want to go back.

"He was here because he had been injured by a blast from a roadside bomb in France and awoke with amnesia. He didn't remember his name, much less his family or where he came from.

"He was told that he had a fiancé in America, but of course he could not remember her and therefore did not love her, or at least he did not remember loving her. So, falling in love with me did not give him a feeling of guilt nor did it make me feel guilty. He simply had no knowledge of the girl.

"He told me he was returning home to tell her about us and would come back to me. Things happened where he could not live up to that promise.

"Jonathan, when I received his letter telling me that he was going to be married in spite of being in love with me, I decided that I could not tell him that I was carrying his child."

216

Jonathan sat up straight in his chair.

"Son, that soldier is Jason Alexander and you are that child that I was carrying."

Jonathan could not breathe. His face was paralyzed in disbelief. He sat back into his chair and looked down at the table not knowing what to say.

"Please don't hate me," Maggie pleaded. "I was afraid I would hurt so many people, Jason's parents, Amy's parents and most of all, Amy. I just could not do that to all of those wonderful people.

"Now that you are going off to war, I feel compelled to let your father know."

"Your husband is my father," Jonathan replied strongly.

"I know, son. Leslie will always be your father, but Jason is your biological father and he has every right to know that his son is going off to war. Also, I know he will love you as a son. I want him to know."

"This is a lot for me to absorb," said Jonathan as he scratched his head. "I need some alone time."

He left and got into his car and headed to town.

***

217

Jonathan went into a local bar and ordered his favorite drink. He sat at a corner table and sipped the drink slowly as he thought about everything that his mom had just told him.

Jason, my father's best friend is my real father, he thought to himself. *I can't be upset with him. He never knew. He will be just as surprised as I am. I feel so sorry for him. Both of us were denied a father and son relationship. And my father is my stepfather, I guess. I love him so much. He has been like a real father to me. This is all so confusing.* He took another drink and his thoughts went silent.

***

The British army was sending Jonathan to New York where he would resign and then enlist into the United States army. Leslie had arrived home the day before and Maggie told him that she had something to tell him. They sat down with Jonathan and she told Leslie that she had told Jonathan about his natural father because Jonathan was heading off to war. Then, she told him the part that Leslie was not aware of, Jason Alexander was the father.

Leslie was beyond shocked. He could not believe that this world was so small that he and Jason would be in the same industry after the war and become close friends. This was very hard to accept. "Blimey! Never in a million years would I have believed this."

He gathered himself and turned to Jonathan. "Son, if it has to be, there could not be a better father than Jason. For that, I am happy. As for you learning that I am not your real father, it truly saddens me. I wish that I were that father."

"You will always be my father," Jonathan replied as he reached over and hugged Leslie.

Maggie was overwhelmed with this display of emotion between the two of them. She suddenly felt so guilty.

"I need to call Jason and tell him," she interrupted them.

"No, Mum. I am going to New York and I will receive a few days liberty before shipping out. I will catch a train to Easton and tell him in person."

"What if he isn't home, Jonathan? He may be out of the country," she questioned him.

"He is home," Leslie reported. "He just left Milan for New York yesterday. We keep in touch with our schedules so that we can get together whenever possible."

That is so weird, thought Jonathan. *But then, neither one knew the truth.*

The three of them headed to the army base and said their goodbyes. Maggie's goodbye was extremely difficult. She could possibly be telling her son goodbye for the last time.

She and Leslie stood with arms around each other as they watched Jonathan walk through the entrance to the base. She laid her head on Leslie's shoulder and cried.

***

Jonathan arrived at Fort Dix in New Jersey just outside New York where he would be reassigned from the British army to the U.S. army as part of the training forces in the 2nd platoon, A company, 5th Battalion, 3rd Brigade.

A Vietnam village was established for training purposes preparing these soldiers for deployment to Vietnam.

Jonathan walked into headquarters wearing a British uniform and would be in a U.S. army uniform within the day.

***

The training was brutal, but Jonathan was more than prepared to accept it. He knew he was planning for this his entire life. The Americans cut up with him about his accent on occasion, but were actually quite fond of him. He gave them everything he had and they could tell he was there for the right reason. Actually, they had also joined, so he was there on a mission in their minds.

**

He received a few days leave before being shipped out and caught the train for Easton. He was more nervous about telling Jason and Stella than he was about training for action in Vietnam.

Stella…it just hit him that she was his sister. *Strange*, he thought. *I was actually starting to have romantic feelings toward her. Oh, my gosh! That would have been awful!*

**

He got out of the cab and walked up to the front door and rang the doorbell. Stella opened the door in disbelief.

"Jonathan," she shrieked. "What..." she stopped. "Is that a U.S. army uniform? What are you doing here and what…"

Jonathan interrupted her, "Hi Stella. Yes, this is U.S. and I will explain inside. Where are your mom and dad?"

She grabbed him by the arm and led him inside. She was so excited to see him again. She wanted to get to know him better and maybe something would come of their relationship. *What in the world was he doing in that uniform?*

Jason and Amy were in the den watching television. They rose from their chairs in disbelief.

"Jonathan, what on earth?" questioned Jason.

"I will explain," Jonathan said as they shook hands.

"Hello, Jonathan," said Amy. "Have a seat, please."

Jonathan sat down among three very inquisitive persons eager to understand his arrival and the reason for this American uniform.

"Well, I have always wanted to do something special. I always felt that there was something waiting for me that was larger than life and the more I watched you Americans go into Vietnam and the longer I watched my government stay out of the fight, the more determined I became to take part.

"I read about a way to get into the U.S. army by way of the British army and after a tour of duty I could then re-enlist in my original outfit. That is what I have done."

"So, that is why you were so inquisitive about Vietnam the last time you were here," Jason questioned.

"You look very handsome in your uniform, Jonathan," Stella blurted out.

"Yes, you do," followed her mother. "We are very proud of you, but I bet your mom is just beside herself with worry."

"Yes, ma'am, she is. I wish I hadn't given her such a shock, but I was determined to do this and I believe she accepted my decision before I left. My father was proud for me, but scared at the same time."

"We totally understand," replied Jason.

"There is more," Jonathan continued. "Could we speak alone, Jason?"

"Why certainly, Jonathan. Girls, would you excuse us?" Jason motioned to them with a brush of his hand.

The girls left with curious expressions on their faces hesitating to leave, but willing to abide by their guest's wish.

Jonathan leaned forward to bring himself closer to Jason so as not to allow the ladies to hear.

"This is going to be a real shock to you just as it was to me when I was told only three weeks ago." He hesitated, wiped his brow and then continued, "Mum told me a story about a young soldier in the second world war that she fell in love with."

Jonathan had Jason's full attention now.

"She told me the full story of your amnesia and your change of heart when you reached America and how you both still loved one another. Then, she told me something that she never told either one of us. She was pregnant with your child. I am your son."

Jason tried to understand what Jonathan was saying, but it sounded too questionable to fathom. Surely, he was not hearing what he thinks he is hearing. There must be a mistake.

"Jonathan, please repeat what you just said. Did you say that I am your father?"

"Yes, sir."

Jonathan did not know what to say or how to react. He sat there staring at this young man trying to determine what had just been told to him and he was having trouble accepting it.

"Why on earth would she keep that from us?" he asked.

"She didn't want to destroy something you and Amy had built for many years between yourselves and with both of your parents. She also worried that if she told me it would damage my self image and the rumors at school would circulate and cause me grief."

"Bless her heart," Jason sighed. "She has kept this to herself for almost twenty-three years. How difficult that must have been for her."

Suddenly, Jason smiled. "So, you are my son? Wow, I have a son! I can't believe it," he exclaimed as he stood to embrace his child.

The two men stood there with arms around each other embracing for what seemed an eternity trying to catch up on all the hugs they missed over the past two decades.

Finally, the men parted and Jonathan asked Jason what he should call him.

"What do you call Leslie?"

"I call him Father."

"Then, how about you call me Dad? Would that be a problem for you?"

"No…Dad, not at all."

"I want to tell my sister now, but I didn't know what to do about Amy. This could cause problems for your marriage."

"I had no memory of Amy when your mom and I met, so hopefully she will understand, especially when she considers the fact that I chose to stay in our relation after determining all the factors and people involved. Surely, she will accept you. I know she has high regard for you anyway."

Amy has always thought that Jonathan was her lover's son and now she was about to be told that he was her husband's son. Her situation continues to be complicated.

"Amy…Stella." Jason called out. "Please come in here.

"Sit down girls. You will not want to hear this standing up."

Jonathan began telling the story as best he could. Each family member had different facial expressions. Stella had one of disappointment because she had feelings for this young man that were beginning to be physical, then a change of expression realizing he was her brother and what a great gift that would be since she grew up an only child.

226

Amy on the other hand had a look of ambiguity at first, then a look of disappointment and followed by a look of total confusion with the situation that she found herself in.

Amy could not bring Leslie into the equation. She needed to be respectful in her actions right now to make this all work for everyone.

She stood and reached out for Jonathan. He rose and they hugged. "My step-son," she remarked.

"Well, do I call you Mum, mom, or Amy? he laughed.

"Just continue to call me Amy," she mused.

Jonathan had two days to say his goodbyes. He hoped to make the most of it. There was so much he wanted to know about his new family. He was both excited and perplexed. He loved his father in England and did not want to hurt him.

Of course, Leslie was bothered by who the father was more than the fact that Jonathan had another father. He already knew that and was prepared for Jonathan learning of that one day.

***

Jonathan and Jason decided to go to the club and play golf. Jason was anxious to see if the doctors were correct and he would remember how to play even though he could not remember ever playing.

Jonathan just wanted time with his dad.

They arrived at the club and the head pro greeted Jonathan and thanked him for serving his country with such valor. He had been an assistant pro when Jason played there in his teens.

Jonathan was impressed. He had not heard any of the stories about his dad's duty in the world war. He wanted his dad to tell him everything he could while they were playing.

They stepped on to the first tee and Jonathan hit a pretty good ball straight down the fairway. He had played golf in college.

"Impressive, son…do you mind my calling you son?"

"Not at all, Dad."

Jason stepped up to the tee. His posture was correct, his alignment was dead on and he put his weight squarely in the middle of his feet with just a little more weight on his forward foot. Everything was correct.

He took the club back and down in a single plane as he had been taught in his youth. Most golfers of that period used the two plane swing. His instructor was ahead of his time.

There was a golfer in Canada that most people would not be aware of until much later even though he had already won dozens of professional tournaments who used the single plane to perfection by the name of Moe Norman. One day he would be a legend among golfers around the world.

Jason out drove his son by thirty yards even though he was more than twice Jonathan's age. He could barely believe that he was sub consciously remembering his swing. He even remembered the "sweet spot". He did not remember that name, but remembered the feel of the sweet spot. This was the meeting of the clubface with the ball while the club was square to the target.

As they played, Jonathan started asking questions.

"Dad, tell me about your youth. I want to know about where you went to school, what you studied, did you have a lot of girl friends...just anything you can tell me that will allow me to know you better."

Jason reminded him that he had no memory and Jonathan apologized. As for his son, he already knew most of those things about him through Leslie.

They finished and went to the nineteenth hole where they continued their history lessons over drinks, both ordering Jack Daniel's black label and coke.

Back home, the girls were waiting anxiously to see how things went with their men. Jason told them that they had a splendid time and Jonathan shared all the details of his life that he could remember.

Stella figured it was her time next, but her dad said that the three of them needed to spend the rest of Jonathan's time together as a family.

Everyone agreed.

For the next two days the three of them tried their best to soak in all twenty-two years and twenty years respectfully of Jonathan and Stella's lives.

There were a lot of tears and even more laughter. Some of the stories were embellished as people will tend to do, but all in all the three of them felt real comfortable with each other at day's end.

It was time to go. Jonathan gave his dad a huge embrace and it lasted for some time as Stella watched holding back her tears. It was her turn and she pulled her big brother into her fold snuggly and lovingly as she told him how she felt about him.

It was a beautiful moment.

This could possibly be the last time any of them ever saw him again…

Chapter 41*Delta

1968 would be the deadliest year in the Vietnamese War with over 16,000 American troops losing their lives and nearly 29,000 South Vietnamese troops along with over 200,000 Viet Cong and North Vietnamese Communists.

Jonathan found himself right square in the middle of the Delta amongst the marshes, swamps, bush, jungles and rice paddies. He hated the rice paddies the most. He stayed wet all the time and the leeches in the fields and in the marshes clung to his skin from his chest down to his legs. The elephant grass growing in the marsh with its sharp edges would cut him as he waded through it, his feet sticking in the deep mud at the bottom. The mosquitoes and the gnats were secondary to the leeches but still were a constant annoyance.

Marching over hills with back packs after plowing through the marsh was a reminder of how out of shape you were. If you did not stay up with the others you were left behind.

He had not seen death yet, but knew it was around the corner.

His platoon arrived at a small village of huts and rice fields with small children running around playing while the elders worked the fields.

Suddenly, the soldier walking next to him let out a yell as a bullet caught him in the chest. Jonathan went down with him looking first for the shooter and then yelling for a medic.

Spontaneous firefight broke out as Charlie was spotted in the thicket surrounding the village. Charlie was the name given to the enemy by American G.I.'s. The surge continued for several minutes until the final shot rang out and all was quiet except for the moaning of the wounded.

Three GI's were dead and seven wounded while two Cong were killed in the hail of bullets. Jonathan did not know if he killed or wounded Charlie or not. He was just happy that he was not hit and was shaking from his first encounter with battle. The soldier next to him was one of the mortally wounded. Jonathan prayed over him.

"Dear Lord, bless this man's family and guide them through the pain that lies ahead. He died valiantly. In the name of the Father, the Son and the Holy Spirit. Amen."

He lay there that night wondering why they were there. These people had been fighting for over a hundred years and there seemed to be no solution to the grievances on both sides. Had he made a bad choice in joining? Was this a senseless war? He told himself it was way too early for him to be making those kinds of judgments. Some of these men had been here for several years. He needed to hear what they had to say.

He was in his second week and had seen battle on three occasions already. The sight of blood and death was still weighing heavy on his heart. He was warned of the small kids inthe villages that were capable of killing you by various means. He prayed that he did not have to shoot a child.

They were on ambush patrol after being told of a threat in the next village and that there may be an entire regiment of Cong nearby. As they drew near you could hear a pin drop. The soldiers crouched along with their weapons at waist high and their eyes focusing all around.

Suddenly, machine gun fire burst from the inside of a thatched hut where Charlie was waiting to set the trap followed by his troops advancing from the surrounding marsh.

Jonathan was firing at will not knowing where the enemy was for sure, only knowing that the men around him were in trouble.

Suddenly, a Vietnamese soldier came charging toward the G.I. next to him with fixed bayonet. Jonathan lunged in front of the soldier to protect him and caught the bayonet squarely in his left side, but despite the penetration of the weapon Jonathan grabbed Charlie by the head and twisted until his neck snapped.

By that time, the firefight was over and the enemy was in retreat due to a gallant effort from Jonathan's company.

The soldier that he protected and saved from a possible death from a bayonet was yelling for a medic and went down on his knees to press and hold Jonathan's shirt stuffed into the wound.

He continued to yell for the medic who eventually arrived after adhering to the needs of several others. The unnamed soldier kept asking if Jonathan would be okay, but the medic would only say that he was doing all he could do for him.

Chapter 42*War Hero

Jonathan woke up in a hospital in South Vietnam. He was wrapped in bandages around his chest covering the work the doctors had done on his incision from the bayonet. He was feeling no pain because of the morphine they had given him and wanted to get up. The nurse stopped him right away.

"You are a very sick soldier, young man and need your rest. You will be able to get up in a few days. There was a lot of damage to your side."

"Thank you, nurse."

"There is a reporter from the states that wants to talk to you," the nurse continued. "I told him it would have to wait a couple of days."

"Why does a reporter want to talk to me?"

"You're a hero, soldier!"

"I don't know what you are talking about, nurse."

"You put yourself in harm's way to protect your fellow soldier. You already are singled out around here having that English accent in an American uniform. So, when you do something heroic as you did everybody knows about it."

"He would have done the same thing for me," Jonathan said humbly.

Two days passed and Jonathan was allowed to get up and walk. The other wounded soldiers in recovery gave cheery salutations as he passed by. There was talk of a medal.

The reporter from New York was waiting for Jonathan when he returned to his bed. "Hello, soldier. "How are you feeling today?"

"I am doing very well, thank you for asking."

"Would you mind giving me a statement for the folks back in America? You being a Brit and saving an American life is a big story. I mean, any soldier doing what you did is news, but this is even more meaningful to the readers."

"There's not much to tell, sir. I saw Charlie heading for the G.I. and did what I had to do. I guess you don't think about danger to yourself when a fellow soldier is in trouble."

"That simple statement soldier is exactly what I was hoping you would say," the reporter smiled. "Word is, you are going to get the Distinguished Service Cross. Reports say you are the first non-American to be honored with that high award."

"Wow! I don't know what to say except my mum will be proud."

"Of course, you speak of your mom back in England. What about your dad? Is he still living?"

"Yes, sir. My dad is an American living in Connecticut," Jonathan said proudly.

"Oh, wow! The reporter exclaimed. "That even makes for a better article. It reminds me of 'A Connecticut Yank in King Arthur's Court' only in reverse. You, my lad are Sir Galahad fighting to protect the Yank in Connecticut. What a great story!"

"I read the novel in college," replied Jonathan "and it is not the same thing."

"Oh, you and I know that but it makes for a great storyline….Sir Galahad from England in an American uniform fighting to protect his Connecticut Yank dad. King Arthur would be proud."

Jonathan looked embarrassed.

***

With the seriousness of the wound the army sent Jonathan back to the states where he would receive a medical discharge from the army and then re-enlist in the British army. Then he would decide whether or not to stay in the military or go back to civilian life.

He arrived in New York to fanfare. The article by the news reporter in South Vietnam had been a sensation. Even those who did not have any idea what the novel mentioned was, they got just enough from the story to raise the young soldier upon a pedestal.

After settling in to the barracks he was informed that the U.S. government was going to pin a medal on his chest the following day. There would be generals and dignitaries and a crowd of civilians. Jonathan was as nervous as he had ever been.

The ceremony took place in an open airfield. Civilians were to one side and officers and enlisted men to the other. Jonathan stood proudly as the four-star general came face to face with him.

"Soldier, we of the United States army are proud to honor you today with the Distinguished Service Cross, the second highest medal awarded to a soldier for service above and beyond the call of duty. Whereas you, Jonathan Chapman, corporal in the United States army did distinguish yourself by protecting the life of a fellow soldier without concern for your own safety."

The general pinned the medal upon Jonathan's chest.

"I salute you." The general came to attention and saluted Jonathan.

Jonathan abruptly returned the salute and said, "Thank you, sir."

***

Upon exiting the train in Easton, Connecticut Jonathan could hear the band playing and the people yelling his name.

The mayor was standing on the platform in front of the crowd and alongside him were Jonathan's dad, step mother and sister who were shedding tears.

The mayor made a speech and then Jonathan's family took turns hugging and kissing him. He had to fight his way through the crowd of cheering onlookers yelling, "Sir Galahad!"

241

"We are so proud of you, son," Jason spoke for the entire family. Stella simply could not take her eyes off of her brother. She admired him so much.

They would spend the next couple of days together and then Jonathan would have to return to camp where he would be shipped home to England.

Chapter 43*Mum's Arms

Jonathan returned to London where he re-enlisted in the British army to fulfill his obligation. His company commander praised him for his historic medal award as did all the men in his company.

As soon as he got liberty he headed to Torrance to spend time with his mom and step dad.

They were awaiting his arrival with anticipation. He walked up to the door and they both fought to get their arms around him.

"Oh, Jonathan," his mom cried. "I am so proud of you and so thankful to the Lord for bringing you home to us."

"Same goes for me, son. I prayed for you and when I heard about the injury it broke my heart."

"Thanks, Father. I needed your prayers over there. Everything will be fine now. I got my taste of war and did what my heart wanted me to do. I believe I got it all out of me and I can move on with my life."

"Thanks for still calling me Father," Leslie grinned appreciatively.

"You will always be my father. Jason is my dad. Having two of you makes me very special in my book."

"Amen," said Maggie.

"How did Jason react," asked Maggie.

"Totally shocked, but very thankful to have a son. Also, he said he could appreciate how hard it must have been for you to contain that secret all these years. And, I now have a sister! How cool is that, Mum?"

Leslie gritted his teeth. He felt very small at this point.

"Well, she is a lovely girl, son and I am so glad you two could spend some time together. How wonderful that you and your dad and sister could be together," Maggie said with a smile.

"Dad said he didn't want to talk to you on the phone about me. He would rather wait until you two can be face to face. He has a lot of questions for you, for both of you."

"He will be in London next month following a trip to Paris," reported Leslie. "We can have him out to the house then."

"That would be great. I will try and get some liberty."

Chapter 44*Mum and Dad

It was January of 1969. Maggie and Jason were both forty-eight years of age. Maggie would be forty-nine in May and Jason would be forty-nine a month earlier. Neither one had changed drastically. Jason had a few gray hairs on his temple. Maggie had a few wrinkles in her brow that were not there in her twenties.

Leslie had brought Jason and Jonathan from London to his home to spend some time with Maggie. As soon as their eyes met, Maggie began to cry and apologize to Jason. She began to explain and he interrupted her telling her that he did not need an explanation. He only wanted to spend some time with her and catch up on his son.

"Jonathan," started Leslie, "why don't you and I run into town and have an ale and let these two have some privacy."

"What a marvelous thing for you to say, Leslie," smile Maggie appreciatively.

"That is rather nice of you, Father," agreed Jonathan as they headed for the door."

"Thank you, Leslie," Jason said as he reached out for Leslie's hand.

"We just might make those two ales," smiled Leslie.

Jason watched as his son got into the passenger side of Leslie's car and the two men rode off for town. He turned toward Maggie and motioned for her to come to him. She walked over slowly as he put his arms around her and pulled her close to him. They stood silently like that for several moments.

"You know I would have made a different decision back in forty-five if I had known."

"I know you would, Jason. But, it is too late to look back. However, I know in my heart that we should have been together all these years. We belong together. I have never stopped loving you."

"Kiss me, Maggie. Kiss me like it was 1945. I need to feel your lips one more time."

Maggie put her warm lips to his and it was like they were back at the beach on that sunny day following the war. It was a long and sensual kiss, one that had been lying in wait for almost twenty-four years.

Neither wanted to stop. There passion was stirring and their emotions were intertwined. It was Maggie the young school teacher and Jason the G.I. all over again. They were trying to recapture the magic they once had.

Slowly, Maggie pulled away. "We must stop, darling. I believe we needed that, but now we must get back to being Jonathan's mom and dad, two sensible people with loving spouses that don't deserve this from us."

"I am tired of doing what is right for everyone else," Jason complained. "I need you so and it keeps me up at night thinking about it. I know you have a wonderful husband and I have a terrific wife, but throughout this masquerade we are simply cheating ourselves from real happiness."

"I'm sorry, Jason, more than you know."

"I know, my dear. I know," Jason said as he backed away.

They quietly waited for Leslie and Jonathan's return. They would spend the rest of the evening sitting and talking about Jonathan's past. Jason listened to every word that Maggie spoke. He wanted to know everything, everything that he had missed.

Jonathan had to get back to his base. Jason hugged Maggie and thanked her for filling in the blanks. The three men left for London.

He and Jason hugged and said their goodbyes. Jason thanked Leslie for everything and got out of the car to enter his hotel. It had been a thoroughly enjoyable day.

Chapter 45*Accident

It was a cold and icy day in Easton, Connecticut. Stella and two of her friends were out having drinks at a local tavern and flirting with the young men that kept staring at them. The girls were not interested, but enjoyed the thrill of adventure. They probably had too much to drink on this night when the streets are treacherously dangerous.

They piled into their car and headed for another club where just maybe the men would be more interesting. They were laughing and remembering the looks on the young men's faces in the previous club when out of nowhere a truck crossed their path sending their car flying into the air and landing on its side.

Stella was unconscious when the ambulance arrived. She had been sitting in the passenger seat referred to as the shotgun seat. The other two girls were in shock and bleeding, but would be found later to not be seriously injured.

The ambulance crew put Stella on a stretcher and put her inside their vehicle while the other two girls who were still mobile were taken by a second ambulance to the same hospital.

249

Once inside the ambulance, the paramedics tried to stop the excessive bleeding to her right leg. It looked like it had been crushed, but they would have to wait to see if any bones were broken or not. They just continued to tie off the bleeding with standard procedures available. She had lost quite a bit of blood prior to their arrival.

Once inside the operating room, doctors put a permanent stop to the bleeding and began the process of determining the seriousness of the leg.

Information was retrieved from the other girls and a call was put in to Jason and Amy. Jason had just returned from Milan and was ready for some time at home.

The phone rang at the Alexander residence and Jason answered. It was the hospital calling to tell of the accident. Jason kept asking questions, but the caller could only say that he and his wife needed to come to the hospital. The doctors there would explain everything to them.

Jason sped to the hospital running red lights when necessary and passing cars at dangerous speeds. Amy was scared to death, but she knew better than to say anything to Jason.

They arrived and ran into the emergency room where Jason began asking for his daughter. They told him to calm down and they would send a doctor out to see him and his wife right away.

The OR doctor came out and asked them to be seated. "Are you the parents of Stella Alexander?"

"Yes, doctor. Please tell us how she is doing," asked Amy.

"She is stable. She has lost a lot of blood. She was involved in an auto accident and her leg was pretty badly injured, but it doesn't look like there are any broken bones. She may have trouble walking for awhile after leaving here, but that may be for some time. Right now, we need to give her a blood transfusion. Since she is unconscious we need your permission to give her donated plasma."

"I will gladly give her my blood," Amy interrupted not wanting to give Jason a chance. "We don't want to use hospital blood. Sorry, Doctor but there just isn't enough evidence on the safety of donated blood."

"No way will I let you do that, Amy. I will give her blood," Jason demanded.

"No, Jason. I insist. Please. Let me do this for my little girl."

"Okay," the doctor interrupted, "Normally, we would do the transfusion while she is in the operating room, but since the paramedics did a great job of stopping the bleeding, she has not lost enough to necessitate an immediate transfusion. Otherwise, there could be serious complications by waiting. Since she has only lost the minimum amount that would require a transfusion, we can wait. Some victims of auto accidents can require as many as one hundred pints of blood. Your daughter only needs a few pints.

"Now, it takes five days to analyze and process designated blood, so if one of you is going to be the donor, let's get started.

"Do you happen to know your blood type?" the doctor asked.

"Yes, doctor. I am B negative."

252

"I'm sorry, Mrs. Alexander, but your daughter is A positive and will not accept your blood type. We will have to use Mr. Alexander? One parent is always compatible."

"Can you come with me Mr. Alexander? We will need to do a lab test on you."

"Sure. Amy, wait for me here. It shouldn't take long. Right, doc?"

"No, it won't take long at all."

Amy was scared to death of the outcome. All she could do was hope Jason was compatible. Even then, that would not prove him to be the father. Leslie and Jason might have the same blood type.

Jason followed the doctor down the hall to a lab and the doctor told the lab tech to draw the gentleman's blood and get him a report as soon as possible.

"Please sit down, Mr. Alexander. I will get with you again as soon as we get back this report."

The blood work was sent to another department with a "rush" order and Jason waited in the office next to the lab.

After about thirty minutes, the doctor returned.

"Mr. Alexander, did you adopt Stella?"

With a very inquisitive expression on his face, Jason replied, "Of course not. Why do you ask such a question?"

I didn't want to say anything in front of Stella's mother and I wanted to be sure that you were the correct blood type."

"The reason I ask is that Stella is A positive. Her mother says she is B negative. Therefore, Stella's biological father must be A or AB. There is no way her father can be a B blood type which is what you are. So, since you are in fact type B, your wife has to be type A or AB, not B as she says.

"So, Amy must be type A or type AB then, Doc. It is a simple mistake on her part. We will get a lab report on her and go from there, huh? Then, when we show her that she is A or AB, she can then do the transfusion for our daughter. Let's get on with it. Our daughter needs us."

"There is no rush. As I said earlier, it usually takes five days or longer to go through all the necessary procedures. It takes longer if many more pints are needed.

"Please go to your wife and have her come down to the lab and we will resolve this matter."

"Thanks, Doc."

Jason went to Amy and asked her to go to the lab. The doctor wanted to do a lab sample on her.

"I thought he couldn't use my type?" she asked.

"He said that he wanted to make sure it was B as you said because he couldn't use mine. We don't want her to have to get a stranger's blood if we can help it."

"Okay, I will go do it," she responded with a worried look on her face. She was terrified of what was happening. Could this be the end of her twenty-one year secret?

Another half hour passed and the doctor sent a nurse to get Jason. She led him to the doctor's office where the doctor was sitting behind a desk with lab work in front of him.

"Sit down, Mr. Alexander. I'm afraid I have some disappointing news for you."

Jason took a seat.

"Your wife is type B just as she stated. I am afraid that you are not Stella's biological father. I'm sorry to be the bearer of this news."

"There has got to be some mistake, doctor. Stella is our child. I know she is."

"Mr. Alexander, it is an impossibility for you to be the father of that young woman. I have the results right here in front of me if you want to see them."

Jason went over to the desk and listened as the doctor pointed out the different blood types of Stella, Amy and himself. It was right there in black and white. He could not possibly be Stella's dad.

He sat back down in a slump. He looked like a beaten man.

"Once again, I am sorry, sir. I will leave you here to catch your breath. We need to move on with the transfusion. Please tell me what you want to do as soon as you can."

Jason did not respond. He simply put his hands to his face and began to think back to all the years he had been with Stella.

Then, his mind wandered to all the possibilities of who the father could be. Finally, it hit him that Amy had been unfaithful to him.

How could she do that and with whom? He had to consider how to handle this. His first priority was Stella. She was the innocent one here. He must take care of her before bringing this issue to Amy. He would deal with her in time.

He went to the doctor and informed him of his decision. He wanted the hospital to use donated blood for their daughter and he appreciated the doctor telling him of the unprincipled dilemma he has found himself in.

The doctor told him how sorry he was to be the one to tell him and hoped he and his wife could resolve the situation. Then, the doctor asked Jason to get Amy's permission to go ahead with donated blood.

Jason approached Amy in the waiting room. "They can not use either of our blood types. I need your permission to let them use donated plasma for Stella.

"Of course, Jason, but I don't understand," she replied shamelessly.

"I don't either, Amy."

Amy did not want to continue the conversation. She wondered if maybe Jason did not know that at least one parent should have the correct blood type. Maybe his amnesia lost that information and if she never mentioned the subject again it would just go away.

She prayed that it would.

Jason asked the doctor if they could go in and see their daughter now. The doctor told the nurse at the station to send them to Stella's recovery room.

They walked in to find her asleep from sedation. She had bruises on her face and arms, but they were told that they were minimal and would probably not leave scars. The only problem was her leg which was in a sling and heavily bandaged.

Amy put her arm around Jason and began to cry. Jason leaned over and kissed Stella on the forehead and gently ran his fingers through her hair. *This was his little girl*, he thought to himself, *regardless of the technical findings.*

They stayed in the room for the most part of an hour. "Why don't you go home now, Amy and get some rest? I will stay with Stella."

"Okay. Will you promise to call if anything changes?"

"Of course I will. There is nothing we can do at this point and the doctor says she is stable."

Amy reached up and kissed him and left the room. Jason watched her walk away and began to wonder who that other man was twenty-two years ago.

Chapter 46*Confrontation

Leslie was in Milan and right in the middle of wrapping up a large buy when he received a message that his hotel had called to inform him that he had an important call come in from the Van Horn sales rep. He had left word for them to reach him at this store if a VIP call came for him.

He knew it was Amy and hurriedly finished his purchase and left for his hotel.

***

Once there, he approached the desk and asked for the number. He went up to his room and made the call. Amy answered. She was home alone and had some very good and very bad news for him.

"Honey, I can tell you now without reservation that you are Stella's biological father."

"Are you sure, Amy?"

"Yes, absolutely sure."

"I am so excited, Amy. I finally have my own flesh and blood child. I think of Jonathan as my own, but this is a different feeling.

"How did you find out?"

"That is part of the bad news. First, Stella was in a wreck," she started.

"What?"

"She is okay, Leslie. The doctors say she will be just fine. We have been with her and she is under sedation. They are going to do a blood transfusion. She lost a lot of blood from one of her legs that was badly damaged when the car flipped.

"That is how I know now that you are her father. They tested both Jason and me and neither one of us were acceptable blood donors. As you must know, at least one parent should be acceptable. Since neither one of us was, that means you have to be her father."

"Oh crap! That means Jason knows."

"I'm not sure about that. He hasn't said anything to me and just maybe his amnesia blocks his knowledge of those facts. We can hope."

"How are you going to handle this?"

"I will just not bring it up again like it is an every day occurrence. Maybe we can get away with our secret for another twenty-two years. Of course, now we know for sure. Before, it was just an educated guess."

"I'm just glad to finally know for sure, Amy. It even makes me feel closer to you. We should think about being together with our daughter. Is that something you would consider?"

"It entered my mind, but I don't think I can do that to Jason nor to Stella. Let's just hope he doesn't discover the truth. If he does know there is another man involved I will have to tell him it is you."

"Oh, my God, my best friend! What will happen to our friendship?"

"Let's not think about it until it comes up. I will see you in Paris next month.

"I love you, Leslie."

"I love you, too."

***

Jason came home to eat and change clothes. Amy was busy in the kitchen preparing him something. He had called to let her know he was coming. She was very anxious as to how the evening would go. She prayed he would not mention the blood test again.

"Hi honey. Dinner will be ready in a moment. Can I fix you a bourbon and coke?"

"That sounds good. It has been a long day."

"How does she look, Jason?"

"No change. Doctors say she will more than likely be awake tomorrow. I am very eager to talk with her and tell her how much I love her."

"I will go back with you tomorrow and we can tell her together."

They finished their dinner and went into the den to settle back and watch television. However, instead of turning the set on, Jason told Amy he wanted to talk.

Uh, oh, she thought. *Here it comes.*

"Amy, you seem a little nervous. Is there anything you need to tell me?"

"Oh, it's just Stella. I am so worried about her."

"You sure there isn't something else?"

Amy squirmed in her chair, "No, why do you ask?"

"I was hoping you would come forward with this, but it appears that I am going to have to play the devil's advocate. I know that at least one parent can give blood to their child. Since neither one of us was qualified to do so, that means I am not Stella's father."

Amy sat up in her chair and looked down at the floor.

"Now do you have something to tell me?"

Amy looked up and tried to say something, but the words would not come out.

"Take your time, Amy. It has been twenty-two years since you got pregnant. I can wait another few minutes," he said candidly.

"Jason, first let me say that I love you and have always loved you. However, there was this need in me for something else. I won't go into it, but one day I ran into that something and it got the better of me. He was happily married, but she didn't love him and

264

for that reason he let his guard down. It was all my fault. I was looking for something that I had always dreamed about, not that there is anything wrong with you. You are a special man and we have loved each other most of our lives. This was a different kind of feeling and I needed to take advantage of it."

"Did you ever see him again?"

She thought to herself that she had better just be straight forward. Jason wasn't born yesterday, well actually he was almost born again yesterday with the amnesia…anyway she needed to go ahead and get this off her chest. "Jason, you have had a huge shock already with the discovery that Stella is not yours. Now, I must tell you something else that will surely shock you again.

"Yes, I saw him again and we still see each other whenever we have the opportunity. I'm sorry, Jason. I thought I could live two lives."

"Oh, my God! I married you instead of the woman I loved and stayed with you for twenty-four years out of loyalty and honor. Now, you are telling me that I have been living in an unfaithful marriage all this time. How could you do this to me, to Stella? Do you love this man?"

"Yes, I love the both of you. He loves me and his wife as well. It is a terrible thing, I know. I hope you can forgive us."

"Us? How on earth could I forgive this man, whoever he is. I don't even know him."

"I'm afraid you do, Jason. Get ready for a third shock; Stella's father is the man she thinks of as Uncle Leslie."

That was it. Jason could not take anymore. He almost fell out of his chair in disbelief. *I'm dreaming. Surely, this isn't happening to me. A lifetime of unfaithfulness and she was with the husband of the woman I gave up for her. Oh my God! And with my best friend!*

"That no good, lying, cheating bastard!" Jason was simply beside himself.

Amy started crying, "Oh, Jason. I am so terribly sorry. I don't know what else to say."

"Does he know?"

"Does he know what," she sobbed.

"Does he know about Stella?"

"Yes. He knows now for sure and we both always figured it was his. We just weren't sure."

"Did he know Jonathan was mine?"

"No. Maggie never told him."

"So, let me get this web of deceit straight, Stella has been living with Jonathan's father for twenty-one years. Jonathan has been living with Stella's father for twenty-three years. You didn't know about Stella for sure. You never knew about Jonathan. Leslie never knew about Jonathan's father and he thought he knew about Stella. I have lived with a woman that I don't even know anymore, sort of like the day I married you. I didn't actually know you then because my memory was gone. Maggie has lived with a man she doesn't love while the man she does love has been the faithful husband to his unfaithful wife, and her lover has been unfaithful to his faithful wife.

"Did I cover everything?"

"Yes, Jason," Amy soberly answered.

"Okay, we have to tell Stella once she has recovered well enough to take it. She needs to know that Jonathan isn't her brother. I believe they really liked each other in a more physical way and finding out they were siblings put a stop to that. Not that I want to push that relationship, but I just don't want these lies to continue to flourish.

"She will always be my daughter and hopefully I will always be her father. I know Jonathan feels the same about his step dad. For that reason alone, I will not show my anger toward Leslie out of respect for my son's feelings."

Chapter 47*Tell Stella

Stella was awake and smiling when Jason and Amy walked in her room. They both went over and kissed her on the cheek.

"I love you with all my heart, honey."

"I love you too, Dad."

"How do you feel, baby?"

"I feel really well, Mom. I'm going to be alright as soon as they refill my tank."

Everyone laughed.

"The doctor said they will start the transfusion in three more hours. I must have lost a lot of blood?"

"Well, we don't need to talk about that. Let's just put it behind us and get you home with us. We want you to stay at our home for a few days before you go back to school."

"Thanks, Dad. That would be nice."

"We will take turns staying here with you, honey. Your mom and I will need some rest over the next three days."

About that time there was a knock on the door and all eyes turned to the doorway. There stood Leslie, all six foot four inches of him with a very intriguing look across his face.

"Uncle Leslie!" shouted Stella and then coughed from exerting herself.

Jason and Amy could not move. This scenario was playing out to its fullest and nobody knew what to say or do.

Leslie went to the other side of the bed and leaned over and kissed Stella gently on the forehead and then reached down and took her hand in his. He was overwhelmed by the touch of his natural daughter.

"Hi there my sweet lassie. So good to see you again. Hope you are feeling well."

"I am wonderful, Uncle Leslie. Just so pleased to see you. You must be working New York this week?"

"No, I caught the first plane out of Milan when I heard the news."

"That is so sweet of you. Mom, Dad isn't that wonderful of Uncle Leslie?"

"Just wonderful," Jason snarled. "Hello, UNCLE Leslie," Jason said with emphasis on the uncle. "What an unexpected pleasure this is," staring point blank at his best friend.

"Hello, Jason. It is so good to see you and Amy."

"I'll bet it is," Jason agreed as he glared toward Amy.

"Well, isn't this just one big happy family?" Jason blurted out. "I need some coffee," he finished as he headed for the door.

Leslie walked around to the other side and gave Amy a hug. "How have you been, dear friend?"

"It has been a traumatic few days, Leslie. Nice of you to come all this way."

She reached up and kissed his cheek as Stella smiled at them both.

"Dad seems a little distraught, Mom."

"Yes, honey. He hates to see his little girl in pain," Amy explained as she looked up at Leslie.

"Neither do I," countered Leslie.

"Why don't we let you rest for awhile, honey? Too much excitement is probably wearing you out. We will go join your dad."

271

"Thanks, Mom. See you soon, Uncle Leslie."

"See you soon, sweet girl."

They walked into the waiting room where Jason was having coffee. He did not look up.

"Jason, let's get this out into the open before it becomes a cancer."

"The things I want to say to you Leslie should not be heard by a lady," Jason retorted, "but then I guess she ain't no lady," he said rather sarcastically. "Sorry, Amy. That just slipped out.

"I deserve that, Jason. We both do. Let's get this over with."

"Jason," Leslie started…

"When I want to hear from you I will let you know. Right now, I will do the talking. You and my wife, and I use that term loosely, have chosen to go against everything that is sacred and moral. Maggie and I were kept in the dark for twenty-two years and we didn't deserve it. She has been a great and loyal wife and I have been the same to Amy.

"However, the real ugliness in the matter is hiding all this from Stella. She deserved to be with her father and mother all these years. It should have been brought to light in the beginning and we would have just parted company. I could have spent all those years with my son instead of him living with you," looking at Leslie. "Then, again I got to spend twenty-one years with Stella and that was a blessing.

"Thing is, what do we do now?" he finished.

"I think I should be the one to tell her, Jason. I need her to know that it was totally my fault that you were left in the dark and Leslie should have had the opportunity to be a real father to her. I totally take the blame."

"When you finish," Jason began, "I think Leslie should go in and have time with her. Not for his sake, but for hers. She will need to sort this all out."

"That's good of you, old man," Leslie said in his finest English.

"Not now, of course," interrupted Jason. "We must wait until after the transfusion and know that she is well enough to hear all this."

They both agreed.

"I have one more thing to offer," Leslie began. "Since she can accept my blood, would both of you rather I give it to her than the donation of a stranger?"

"As much as it offends me, I must admit it would be best. They said it takes quite a few days to prepare designated blood, but the doctor says she can wait without any danger. Let's go see the doctor," Jason answered as he started for the hallway.

"Doctor, a lot has transpired since we last talked. This gentleman is Stella's natural father, so I would expect his blood to be type A. If not, this little drama should become a Broadway play."

The doctor could not help but chuckle.

"Anyway, we three have agreed to let the natural father give Stella his blood. So, will you call off the procedure set for today?"

"Of course you all know that means five extra days of waiting. That won't be a problem, but just wanted to put it out there."

"We understand," replied Amy. "We know she is stable and comfortable, and you said earlier it should not present any complications."

They were all in agreement and the doctor left with Leslie to make preparations.

***

Leslie wanted to be there when Stella was given the news of her biological father. He called Maggie and told her that he was in New York on unexpected business and after learning of Stella's accident he wanted to stay and give moral support.

She totally agreed and asked him to wish Stella well for her.

***

Five days went by and Leslie stayed his distance working the Manhattan fashion shops.

Stella received her father's plasma and was doing quite well according to the staff. She asked for her parents.

Jason and Amy joined her in her room and congratulated her on her recovery. She surprised them with a question, "Do you guys know whose blood was given to me?"

They both looked at each other knowing it was too soon to give her the news.

"We will see if we can find out for you, honey," said Jason. "By the way, the doctor says you can leave in the morning. Your wounds are healed enough to let you go home."

"Great, Dad. Am I still going to your house?"

"Yes, your dad and I both think it best."

***

The next morning they all arrived at their home. Amy had called Leslie and told him to meet them there for the grand finale. He was sitting in front waiting to Stella's surprise.

"What is Uncle Leslie doing here?"

"He had told us that he wanted to be here when you got home to celebrate your recovery," Amy replied.

"Well, how nice of him. He is a very special man."

Jason and Amy gave each other a similar look.

"Hi everybody," Leslie waved.

The girls waved back.

Once inside they all settled down in the den. Amy served a glass of wine to Leslie, a beer to Stella, wine for herself and of course a Jack Daniel's black label and coke for Jason.

The mood was somber with everyone worrying about Stella's reaction to the news. Stella noticed and asked if there was something they were not telling her. "Did the doctors give you some bad news?"

"Oh no honey, its just that your dad and I have something to tell you that is very important and we are all struggling with how to say it."

"Then, it must involve Uncle Leslie," she questioned. "Is something wrong with you, Uncle Leslie?"

"Oh no Lassie, old Uncle Les is just fine. I'm as healthy as a horse as you Americans would say."

"Okay, you guys, what is going on?"

They all looked at one another deciding who should break the news. Amy had told them earlier that she would, but now she was chickening out.

"Stella, honey, you know how much I love you," Jason insisted.

"Uh, oh," Stella inserted, "That sounds scary!"

"No honey, nothing scary, just something that we all recently learned and needed to share with you. We think you are old enough at twenty-one to understand and deal with the news."

"Jason, do you want me to do this," asked Amy.

"I will be just fine. Give me a moment."

"Now you guys are really scaring me."

"Okay, I will get to the point," Jason said hurriedly. "We learned from the blood samples taken from all of us that I am not your biological father."

"What?" exclaimed Stella. "But, Dad, that can't be. Of course you are my father. You and Mom had me and brought me home from the hospital over twenty-one years ago. You told me all about it."

"I was completely unaware, Stella. Even your mom was not absolutely sure. She had an affair and we learned last week that another man was the father of that baby girl."

Suddenly, Stella looked over at Leslie. "Oh, man. Wait just one minute here. Don't tell me..." she stopped and looked at her mom and back at Leslie. "It's him, isn't it? The man I always thought of as Uncle Leslie is my birth father."

"Yes, Stella," Leslie jumped in. "I am your father. I'm sorry you had to find out this way, Lassie."

"But, Dad," she cried out as she looked disheartened toward Jason.

"I am still your dad, Stella. I will always be your dad. This man is just the person that fathered you. He's a good man, honey."

Leslie looked shocked.

"Uncle," she hesitated, "Leslie, did you know?"

"No, I didn't. Neither did your mom. We surmised that it was so, but we had no proof and we did not want to say anything to your dad. We were wrong, I know now."

"Oh, sweet Jesus! This can't be happening. Mom, how could you do this to me? You have lived a lie my entire life and look what you have done to my dad. My poor dad doesn't deserve this." She reached out and embraced Jason.

There was a quiet time before anyone said anything.

"Oh, my Lord! What about poor Maggie?" exclaimed Stella.

"She doesn't know," Leslie said looking down in despair. "I have to go home and face her now. That will be even harder than today's unveiling. I truly dread it."

"Of course, I will want to talk to Maggie as well," said Jason, "but I will wait until my next trip to London. That will give her some time to cool down from your dalliances," glancing over to Leslie.

"What happens now?" Stella asked.

"Well, honey there is one more surprise for the three of you. I can not continue to live with your mother."

Amy had a shocked look upon her face.

"Dad, that was over twenty years ago. Can't you forgive her for that now?"

"There is more. I have to tell you this so that you will understand my departure."

Amy interrupted him, "Please, Jason…don't."

"Sorry, but I have to. There is no other way to explain my leaving." He turned to Stella. "They have been romantically involved this entire twenty-two years. I can not live with her knowing that."

"Oh, my God, Mom. How could you?"

"Stella, you probably won't understand this today, but maybe someday you will. I love both of these men, but in different ways. It was wrong, I know, but it happened and your dad is probably right. We need to move on. Your father has asked me to be with him knowing you are his daughter. I wasn't going to do so, but your dad gives me no choice."

"This is just more than I can handle right now. I need another drink," Stella uttered to herself as she went to the bar.

She got halfway to the bar and suddenly shrieked, "Wait!" She turned around. "Jonathan isn't my brother! Hot damn! At least one good thing came from all this," she laughed out loud.

That definitely drove the elephant out of the room.

"What about you, Stella," Leslie asked after a few moments. "What will you do?"

"I still have another year at U Conn. I will be staying in the dorm again. In the summer, I will stay here with mom if she stays in this house. If she goes to Europe to be with you I will stay at my dad's, wherever that will be."

"I think we all need some time to think this through," said Amy.

Everyone agreed and had another drink.

Chapter 48*Admission

Leslie traveled back home bearing the weight of the world on his shoulders. He first must tell Jonathan that Stella is not his sister. Then, he must let Maggie know that he has a daughter.

He called Jonathan at the base in London and asked him to meet him at the airport. Jonathan picked him up and Leslie suggested they go to a pub for an ale. Once there he carried on a lot of small talk trying to work up the courage to tell Jonathan about Stella. He had cheated on Jonathan's mom and Stella wasn't his sister, two gargantuan facts to lay upon his stepson.

"How is the army treating you, Jonathan?"

"Very well, sir. They still call me Sir Galahad and stuff, but its all in fun. I may stay in. I really haven't made up my mind."

"Jonathan, I just flew in from New York where I spent time with Jason, Amy and Stella."

"My sister? How is she doing, Father?" He still called Leslie Father. Leslie wondered if that was going to cease after his revelations.

"She was involved in an auto accident, but she is home and doing fine now. I asked your mum not to tell you because I wanted to do so when I got back. If it had not gone well, naturally we would have told you earlier.

"I flew there the day Amy called and I gave blood for a transfusion to Stella."

"I don't understand, Father. Why didn't one of her parents give blood?"

"Jason was tested and his blood type was not a candidate for giving blood to Stella. They had already learned that Amy was not a candidate."

Jonathan scratched his head. "I don't understand. One of them has to be a suitable fit."

"Fact is, son, Jason is not Stella's biological father."

"Oh, my gosh! Who is?"

"I am."

Stone silence. Jonathan had just recently gone through this with his father, finding out that Jason was his natural father. Did he hear him correctly?

"Come again, sir."

"I am Stella's father. Her mother and I had an affair over twenty years ago and she got pregnant. We never knew for sure until this past week."

"This can't be happening again," Jonathan said. "Surely this is a sick joke. You are not my father, but you are Stella's father. Jason is not Stella's father, but he is my father. For the love of God, what is happening? Am I going to find out next that my mum isn't my mum?"

"I'm truly sorry Jonathan. I know this is all overwhelming to you. I don't know what to say to you. You don't deserve all this. You have been a good son, or step-son. You have been a terrific son to your mum. I'm just beyond words to comfort you right now."

"Well, there is something to this after all. I loved having a sister, but I was feeling a little paranoid about my true feelings for Stella. Now, I can release those feelings. I really do like her."

"As a matter of fact," Leslie began, "After she overcame the news, she was jumping for joy when she figured out that you were not her brother since like you she said she had feelings for you."

"She did? Wow! That is great news. I think I deserve some good news."

"How are you and I?" asked Leslie.

"We are good, Father. You made a mistake, but you have a beautiful daughter…hey, how about a real kicker to all of this? How about if I married Stella? You would be my father-in-law! Isn't that a kick in the head?"

They both laughed.

"Sadly enough, son I must now go tell your mom that I have a daughter. It is a heavy burden I am carrying. She loved Jason all those years ago and married me for your sake and for the sake of Amy and others. Now, she will see that she probably should have gone to the man she loved. You would have been just fine growing up with your mum and Jason. It is just a sad, sad state of affairs… no pun intended."

They parted company on good terms and Leslie caught a cab to his home. When he entered the front door Maggie was standing there with a drink in her hands for him. *What a good wife,* he thought.

"Hi darling," she said as she handed him the drink. "How was your flight?"

"It went well. Our son picked me up at the airport and we went into town for drinks."

"Oh! That was nice. I assume you wanted to tell him about his sister?"

"Yes, I did."

"I guess he was thrilled that she is okay."

"Yes, he was. Can we sit down, Maggie?"

"You must be tired, dear. I know it is a long flight."

"It isn't the flight, Maggie. There is something I must tell you."

"What is it, honey? Is there something about Stella that you didn't tell Jonathan?"

"No. She is doing well and will recover nicely. But, there was something about her that shocked Jonathan. I had to tell him that Stella is not his sister."

"Oh, no! Not again. I don't understand. Who is the father this time? Is Jason upset? Is Stella okay?"

"Slow down, honey. I will try to explain." He began telling her about the blood tests from Jason and Amy and the discovery that Jason could not possibly be the father. When questioned, Amy admitted that she had thought for many years of the possibility that Jason was not Stella's biological father because of an affair over twenty years earlier.

"Maggie, I gave blood for Stella's transfusion. I am her biological father."

Maggie dropped her wine glass.

"This is a nightmare and I am soon going to wake up and it will all go away."

"No, Maggie, it won't. It is true and I am ashamed. Amy and I didn't know for sure and remained silent all these years in the hope that Stella was Jason's daughter. We both feel horrible about our behavior, but the most important thing was Stella and she is going to be fine. I think she accepts me as her father and of course will always love Jason just as Jonathan will always love me."

"Do you realize the magnitude of what you are telling me, Leslie? If I knew back then about you and Amy, I would have gone to Jason and spent the last twenty years with him and our son.

"I married you for the sake of morality and conscience and duty. I did all that for you and Amy and the kids. What a fool I was!"

She started crying. Leslie knew he better just leave her alone right now. He put his hand on her shoulder and told her he would give her some time to herself and went into his bedroom.

Oh, Jason. What have I done? I took away our right to happiness for over twenty years and did it for all the wrong reasons. Forgive me, Jason.

Chapter 49*Reunite

Stella finished her junior year in May of 1969 and had the summer to do with what she pleased. What she wanted was to travel to Europe and be with Jonathan.

She called her father in London and asked him to please have Jonathan call her. She and her new father talked for a few minutes and it appeared that they were going to get along just fine. She asked if she could stay with him and Maggie while there. Of course, he was thrilled that she asked, but was unsure if Maggie would even let him stay at this stage of the game.

"Let me ask Maggie, honey. I told her about you and I am in the dog house right now. I will get back to you.

Leslie went to Maggie and asked if they could speak.

"It's a free world, Leslie."

"My daughter just called. She wants to come and spend some time with us and Jonathan. I was open with her and explained that it was unsure right now whether or not you would allow me to remain in our home. I told her I would ask you."

"Just answer this, Leslie. Did you ever sleep with Amy again?"

"No honey, never," he replied emphatically. He now hated himself even more than he did an hour ago.

"Okay, then. We will put our situation on hold for now and let the kids have some time together. I would enjoy having her stay with us. She is a lovely girl."

"You are one hell of a woman, Maggie!"

***

In a couple of days Jonathan called and Stella answered.

"Hi, Stella."

"Hello, Jonathan."

"So, you are no longer my little sister," he laughed.

"It appears to be that way. Wonder who will be our brother or sister tomorrow?" she kidded.

"I know. Isn't it all just pure madness?"

"I still can't get over your father turning out to be my father and my father is your father. The whole scenario is so astonishing, Jonathan."

"I know. So, what did you need? Just want to talk about all this?"

"No, I was wondering if you would like it if I flew over to London in a couple of weeks to see you."

"Are you kidding? I would love that," he gushed.

"Super! I will get tickets and get back to you. Tell me how to get hold of you at the base."

He proceeded to give her the information and they chatted for awhile before hanging up. They were both excited at the forthcoming time together.

***

Stella stepped off the plane in London to the waves of her father, Maggie and Jonathan. It was a warm, clear day and everyone was dressed casually for summertime .

Stella first walked up to Leslie and gave him a hug and kiss. "Hi Father. Good to see you again."

"Great to see you, Daughter," he grinned.

"Hi, Maggie," smiled Stella. "I guess you are my new step-mom."

"Isn't it crazy, Stella?"

Stella turned to Jonathan. "Hi good looking. Remember me?"

"I most definitely do young lady. You used to be my sister."

"Well, I am just glad everyone is getting a little humor out of all of this," Maggie said sarcastically. "I'm not exactly thrilled with everything that happened." Her eyes turned toward Leslie.

"Okay, everybody, what do you say we go get some dinner." Leslie tried desperately to change the subject.

"I'm starving," Stella agreed and off they went.

***

After dinner Jonathan went back to his base and Stella went to her father's home in Torrance. Jonathan told her he would call her in the morning and if he could get off base he would pick her up.

***

Back at home, Maggie had little to say to Leslie and it gave him some private time to spend with his daughter. She mostly wanted to talk about Jonathan. Leslie could tell there was something special brewing.

He asked her if her dad back in Connecticut had anything nice to say about him.

"Let's just say my dad doesn't hate you. He is just hurt by what you did and continued to do and pretending to be his best friend."

"I have to admit that I wanted to be with him as often as possible to get information about you. I was doing the same thing with your mom. If you were going to turn out to be my daughter I wanted to know everything about you.

"But, I can surely understand how I could never be your dad's friend again after what Amy and I did all these years. I'm just happy that you didn't turn your back on me."

They hugged and Stella decided to turn in. It had been a long day.

***

The next morning Jonathan called Stella after she finished her breakfast and told her that he was given a three day pass for what he called a family emergency. He would pick her up in an hour.

She was so excited knowing he was coming and they would have some quality time together. She told Leslie and Maggie that he was coming and hoped they did not have a problem with her interest in Jonathan. He was still her step brother after all.

"No, Stella. This isn't your typical family situation. You two were not raised together and never even knew about the parental complication. Go have a good time, darling."

"Thanks, Father. How about you, Maggie? He is your son and I am your husband's daughter. Do you have a problem with that?"

"After what all has transpired the past year, nothing can bother me, Stella. Like your father said, go have a good time."

Jonathan came in and hugged his parents and grabbed Stella and left. Maggie and Leslie looked at each other and laughed.

He opened the passenger door for Stella and she got in thinking what a gentleman he is. "Where would you like to go, Stella?"

"How about showing me some of those old castles my mom was telling me about? Then, I would like some crumpets and tea," she laughed.

Crumpets were a bakery item made mostly of flour and yeast and would be similar to the English Muffin served in America.

"Your wish is my command, my lady."

Off they drove and they visited several castles in the countryside which astonished Stella. The magnitude and old English charm of the setting with moats excavated around them and walls reaching into the sky simply fascinated her.

Jonathan told her stories that penetrated from the stone walls of long ago villains and damsels living within, of kings and queens and knights and even Robin Hood and his Merry Men.

It was a glorious day and she was as happy as she had been in her entire life. She wondered if he was feeling the connection that she felt between them.

They were holding hands by the third castle and after touring the long halls they both decided it was time to eat.

They went into London and found a corner bakery where they sat and had their crumpets and tea. She thought they were scrumptious. She ate four of them before she realized.

"What do you say we take in a movie. There is a new film in town from America that everyone is raving about called, "Butch Cassidy and the Sundance Kid.""

"Oh, I love Robert Redford," exclaimed Stella. "And Paul Newman ain't that bad."

"Okay, then. Let's go."

After the movie, they came out with huge smiles across their faces. They loved the movie and would talk about it all the way back home. It was a great escape from the reality that this young couple had been living in.

They pulled up to the front of the house and Jonathan told her that he was not coming in. He needed to get back before the bugle sounded. He started to get out and walk her to the door, but she insisted that he stay in the car and she would let herself out.

Like her mom, she would make the first move and reached over and kissed him goodnight. It was a rather warm and subtle kiss, one that would stay with Jonathan throughout the night.

The next day would be more of the same. Maggie went back in time as she watched her son walk toward the front door in his army uniform to pick up his girl for another day of fun. How she longed for more of those days from a quarter of a century ago.

The young couple spent all three of Jonathan's liberty days together. At night, she got to spend some valuable time with her father. She was so glad she chose to come to England.

On the eve of the third day, she kissed Jonathan goodbye and told him that she would never forget this time they shared together. She would try and come back with her dad or mom the next time they came on business.

"I don't want this to be our last time together, Stella. I will find a way for us to be together again. Take care of yourself and good luck in your final year of school."

***

She stayed another several days with her father and Maggie and then it was back to America to see how things were going with mom and dad.

Chapter 50*Jason Stays

Amy did not want Jason to move out. She wanted things to stay as they were. Naturally, she would have to give up Leslie, but she did not want to lose her husband and her daughter. She realized Stella would go with her dad if there was a choice.

Jason was brooding over his drink and Stella was watching television. Amy was busy in the kitchen. Even though Jason announced that he would be leaving, he was in favor of taking his time to do so. There was a lot to consider.

Stella walked over from her couch to join her dad in the study. She placed her arm around his neck and reached down and gave him a kiss on top of his head.

"You doing alright, Dad?"

"I will be fine, sweetie. I just need to figure this all out."

"You know Dad; if you leave I am going with you."

"I appreciate that, honey, but if your mom does not go away with your father and stays in this house I think maybe you should stay with her. Your mother needs you. Not that I don't, but a woman alone is different than a man out on his own."

"But, Dad, after what she has done, I don't know if I can do that."

"I know, honey. That's why we need to take some time and think of all the ramifications. It will all work out. Let's see what happens."

Amy came into the study. "Do you mind if I join you two?"

"It's a free country, Mom."

"Stella, you don't need to be sarcastic to your mother."

"I'm sorry, Mom. It just hurts awfully when I think of what you did all these years to Dad. He didn't deserve it."

"I agree, Stella. Of course, he didn't deserve it. Your dad is a fine, honest man. He deserves better than me. However, I am asking for forgiveness and a chance to make our family continue to work. I can change.

"Jason, we could start planning our trips together instead of my going to different locations than you. That would prevent you from wondering who I was with all the time. My dad would agree as long as we got the job done."

"So, as long as I have you in my sights you will be faithful?"

"No, Jason. That isn't what I meant. I just think it would be nice to be together more often. We have spent way too much time apart. I am not making excuses for myself, but that had to be part of the reason for what I did. That quote, 'Absence makes the heart grow fonder' is misleading. It makes a person wander."

"It didn't make me wander," Jason candidly remarked.

"Okay, I am digging a hole for myself. I know that. All I can do is try and be as open as I can and hope you two keep me around. I love you both with all my heart."

"What do you think, Dad? Should we keep the old gal around?"

"Stella, you're being sarcastic again." He couldn't help but chuckle.

"Alright you two, I will get out of here and get back to my kitchen and leave you two to your colloquialisms."

Stella and Jason gave each other a wink. It would be awhile before anyone would know what they were going to do.

302

Chapter 51*Making Up

Maggie agreed to give Leslie another chance. After all, she was almost fifty and not interested in the dating game. Leslie was happy on one hand and disappointed on the other with the thought of not being with Amy again. He knew this was for the best. He had been terribly wrong and owed it to this woman of dignity to treat her right this time.

He came home from work with a dozen red roses. Maggie pretended to be happy with the sentiment, but deep down she was still hurting. Funny thing was, she was not hurting so much from Leslie's unfaithfulness, but from the thought again of how she gave up her true love to be with this man.

He tried that evening to seduce her, but she was not even close to being ready for that. He would have to suffer.

She wondered how it was going in Jason's home.

***

A couple of weeks went by and slowly but surely Leslie was back into the fold. He made a point of staying in England for at least a month and taking care of as much business in the area as possible.

He knew that once he went back to France or Italy she would start wondering about him. There was nothing he could do about that. He just needed to be as focused as he could be on her while here and give her all the love and devotion one can possibly bestow upon another.

She was slowly coming around and even found the time to allow him into her bed. It appeared that life would get back to normal for the Chapmans.

Chapter 52*Back to Work

It came time for everyone to get back to work. The Alexanders needed to go to Milan and Leslie needed to go to Paris. It was June of 1970 and would be twenty-five years since Maggie and Jason's romantic holiday on the coast of England. They were both fifty years young now.

Stella was just shy of twenty-two and decided to get out on her own. She found her an apartment in Summers Landing just as her mom had done before she was born.

Jason and Amy were back on good terms and he could not believe that he was staying in this marriage after all she had done to destroy it. However, Jason was the epitome of virtuous and cared deeply for Stella. She needed a stable home life even if she lived fifteen minutes away. They would still be a family.

***

They landed in Milan and went directly to their hotel. Van Horn Milan was the new kid on the block and was extremely successful now. So much so that this was their second trip in a row to Milan. After visiting with the Milan store they would rent a car and drive to Florence taking in some scenery along the way. It was only a three and a half hour drive straight through, but to get a view of the mountains and other scenic pleasures they could avoid Genoa and spend four to five hours traveling which is what they chose to do.

They wrapped up their business in Milan, picked up their rent car and off they headed on their little excursion.

***

Florence was quite beautiful and stood alone as the art cultural center of the world. The works of Italian artists were displayed throughout the many galleries. Perhaps thirty percent of the entire world's most important works of art were in Florence including many of the Madonna paintings, not to mention the magnificent sculptures of Michelangelo, boy wonder.

Jason and Amy were fascinated with this cultural city and its vast inventory of Renaissance art. They spent an entire day devouring every piece of art and sculpture they could see.

It was time for them to take care of business for Amy's father. Much to their chagrin, they needed to part from their vacation and visit the Florence shop.

***

They had a wonderful dinner on the terrace of their room with the moon staring down from above and a warm breeze blowing across their faces. Soft music was coming from down below and they could hear dogs barking in the alley ways.

It grew near time for bed and Amy wanted him. She had not made any advances to this point. She hoped he was ready to put the past where it belonged.

She put on a thin negligee and came out of the bath room looking like she did on the night of their wedding.

Jason was in awe of her sensuality that night. It was captivating to say the least and to the delight of Amy he was all hers.

Chapter 53*Last Straw

Stella was sick and someone needed to stay home with her. Van Horn Paris was having a problem with getting their shipments on time and Jason needed to be there and straighten everything out. It was decided that Amy would stay home with her daughter.

***

Jason kissed Stella goodbye and told her she was in good hands with her mom. He and Amy embraced and kissed and he left the two of them at his home where he knew Stella would be fine.

"Call me in Paris if you need me," he said as he walked out the front door. "I love you gals."

By chance, Leslie was headed for Manhattan which he had neglected for a few months partially because of the situation between him and Jason. He knew through the grapevine that Jason and Amy were needed in Paris, so thought this would be another chance to spend some time with his daughter.

He settled in at the Waldorf-Astoria on Park Avenue. Nothing but the finest for Leslie. He thought maybe he could invite his daughter to join him for dinner in the hotel.

He called Stella's number and there was no answer. He wondered if she was house sitting for her parents. He called their number and Amy answered.

"Amy?"

"Leslie, why are you calling here?" she asked in amazement.

"I thought you and Jason were in Paris?"

"Stella got sick and Jason had to go alone. I'm still wondering why you are calling here."

"I tried Stella's number and there was no answer, so I was hoping I could catch her at your home. It's great to hear your voice."

"I really miss you, Leslie. How are things going with you and Maggie?"

"She has given me another chance. We are doing well."

"Did she ask you if you and I ever saw each other romantically again after that first time?"

"Yes, she did"

"Did you tell her the truth?"

"No. I didn't have the heart to do that. It would have been too much for that sweet lady."

"I understand, darling. So where are you?"

"I'm at the Waldorf."

"You're in New York?"

"Yes. I was calling to see if Stella could join me. How is she doing?"

"She is okay, now. She just had a virus. She is up and around, eating solid foods and actually feeling well enough to be on her own."

"Amy, this is a golden opportunity for us. You are going to be attached at the hip with Jason from now on. We need to take advantage of this opportune moment."

"I was hoping you would say that, Leslie. I have been laying awake nights thinking about you."

"All you have to do is tell Stella that you are going to work Manhattan now that she is well. I want you to join me in the Starlight Roof. Ella Fitzgerald is performing tonight."

"Oh, that sounds wonderful!"

"Is that a yes?"

"Yes. What can I tell Stella?"

"Just tell her you are taking a client to dinner tonight if she asks. How about you leave now and spend the day with me in my room?"

"Sounds wonderful. I am on my way."

***

"Stella, since you are doing well I need to get into Manhattan and get some work done. Will you be okay on your own?"

"Sure thing, Mom. I am going back to my place and will probably go to bed early tonight. Thanks for staying home with me."

"I love you, baby. Just lock the door when you leave."

Amy caught the train to New York. She was as excited as the first time she met with Leslie. *Oh, what a naughty girl I am.*

Leslie opened the door to his hotel room and she threw herself into his arms. "Leslie, darling. I have missed you so much."

311

They began kissing and ripping at each other's clothing as they stumbled their way across the room and into the bedroom. They were half naked as they fell upon the bed and continued to kiss. They would make up for lost time on this day.

"Let's order room service, honey," Leslie said as he reached for the phone. "What would you like?"

"Surprise me, Leslie."

Leslie placed an order and then proceeded to the shower. Normally, they would go together, but he asked her to wait for their order. She could take her shower after him.

A few moments passed and the phone rang. Thinking it may be the food service she picked up the phone.

"Hello," she answered in her distinctly raspy voice.

There was a moment of silence at the other end. Then, suddenly, "Amy, I would recognize that voice anywhere. Well, I am too much of a lady to tell you what I think of you, but I hope the two of you will be very happy together."

"Maggie, wait… the phone went silent.

Amy just stood there, naked, phone in hand, staring at the floor.

Leslie walked in with a towel wrapped around his middle, water dripping from his head. "Was that food service?"

"It was your wife."

"Oh, crap!"

"I know. She immediately recognized my voice."

"What did she say?"

"She said she hoped we would be happy together."

"Well," Leslie sighed, "I guess it is over. Maybe it is for the best. Now, you and I can be together and quit sneaking around."

"I hate to do that to Jason, but then again I don't think it would bother him all that much. I know he still loves Maggie. Maybe this whole scenario played out for the best for everyone?"

"Let's get dressed and go enjoy Ella."

"Why not? The damage is done," Amy agreed.

Chapter 54*Soap Opera

Amy would go home and wait for the return of Jason to put an end to the soap box drama that had been influencing everyone's lives for twenty-five years. She would tell him alone and then go to Stella and lay the news in front of her.

***

Jason returned a week later. He had taken care of business and was ready to spend some time with his wife and daughter before heading to London.

When he walked in the door he found Amy sitting alone in the study with two drinks beside her.

"Here, honey. Welcome home," as she handed Jason his Jack Daniel's black label and coke. "How was your trip?"

"I could have used you, but was able to take care of the problem on my own. Where is Stella?"

"She went home. She is doing just fine."

He sat across from her ready to exchange notes on business. He began filling her in and she complimented the exchange with the work she accomplished in Manhattan during the week. Naturally, she left out the nights spent with Leslie who stayed in town all week and was still at the Waldorf waiting to hear from her about this talk she was about to have.

Finally, she worked up the courage to lay her cards on the table.

"Jason, I want you to know that I have loved you since I was twelve years old and will always love you. That goes without question. I probably haven't shown it by my dalliances throughout our marriage, but I really and truly do.

"With that said, I have to tell you something that will probably necessitate the end of our marriage. Leslie is in town. He wanted to spend time with his daughter and called here looking for her. I answered the phone and told him she had been sick, but was better and after talking a few moments neither one of us could resist seeing each other again.

"I went to his hotel room and while there answered his phone thinking it was room service. It was Maggie calling from Europe and she recognized my voice."

Jason just sat stoically as if nothing she said penetrated his brain. It was becoming old news hearing of the baggage she was carrying.

"I have decided," she continued, "to be with Leslie and give you the opportunity now to be with Maggie if that is what you want. Leslie will surely move out. I will probably join him in London after talking to my dad. I will have to get our working relations settled.

"Again, I am sorry, Jason and regret all the pain we have caused you and Maggie."

Jason just sat there, not in shock, simply in limbo between the real world and the fabricated world he found himself in.

"You know, Amy," as he finally broke his silence, "this just doesn't shock me anymore. I have seen and been a part of so many illusions that this is simply the closing of the final chapter.

"You can have your freedom to be with Leslie. I fell out of love with you when I found out about the two of you the first time. I just hope your daughter will forgive you again."

"Thank you, Jason. No man deserves what you have been through, but especially you. You are a saint.

"As for Stella, I believe that since I will be with the man who fathered her, in time she will grow to accept us as a family and she will never stop loving you. I can assure you of that.

"I don't think you will be joining the three of us as Christmas dinners, but we will work this thing out."

They rose and gave each other a hug.

***

Stella opened the door of her apartment to let her mother inside. Amy had told her she was coming and Stella had tea set up on the dinette table next to the kitchen. They could see the trees of the woods backing up to the apartment and watched as two squirrels chased each other across the back fence.

"Stella, do you believe you could learn to love your father?"

"I have always loved him as an uncle. It will take some time to love him like a father. Not sure if that will ever happen, but it won't be because I don't try."

"That's great, honey because he is going to need your love. He and Maggie are splitting and your dad and I have decided to do the same thing. Your father and I are going to be together in London and your dad will keep the house."

"Holy Moses! This just continues to amaze. So, you're just going to leave me?"

"I knew you would think that first. No, that is not the way it is. Remember, part of my territory is New York. I have London, Paris, Milan, Florence and Manhattan. I should be here every three months year round. I will be in town for at least three weeks. I can spend more time here because I am the boss's daughter," she said laughingly.

"Okay, Mom. I understand. Three months goes by pretty fast and I will have my dad here if I need anything. I have been interviewing for jobs and will probably go to work fairly soon. That will keep me occupied. I would like to get something that requires travel to London so I could see Jonathan," she smiled.

"In this family, who knows what will happen with that situation," Amy laughed.

"I know. Think about it…if I were to marry Jonathan, Dad would be my father-in-law, my father would be Jonathan's

318

father-in-law, Maggie would be my mother-in-law and you would be Jonathan's mother-in-law."

They both started laughing out loud.

Chapter 55*Fresh Start

Leslie called Maggie to give his apologies and to ask when he could come and get his things. She told him she would spend the day out with some girl friends and give him all day to pack.

***

He packed his clothes, a few pictures, some personal belongings and headed for London to move into one of the new modern high rise apartments that were convenient to everything.

Amy would fly in the next day and her belongings would be right behind her.

***

He greeted her at the airport with a huge kiss, both knowing that they no longer needed to look over their shoulder.

He showed her the apartment and she was delighted with the glamour of it and excited to start their new life together.

"Let's break in our new home, Leslie," she giggled.

He didn't hesitate to follow her lead.

"Afterwards they lay in bed and planned their future together. They wanted to marry eventually, but would wait until Stella felt more comfortable around them. They needed her approval if they were going to make a good marriage void of all their transgressions.

They decided to make love one more time…

Chapter 56*Fruition

It was July 16th, 1970, exactly twenty-five years to the day since that night at Maggie's home when she and Jason first made love and expressed their feelings for each other. Jason had planned it this way. He would arrive at Maggie's home on their anniversary date that united them forever with Jonathan.

He wanted everything to be perfect. He had called Maggie's dad and reminded him of whom he was. Her dad remembered quicker than Jason expected because Maggie had told him and her mom everything now that she was alone.

Lionel had told Jason how sorry he and Margaret were that his son was kept from him all these years. They felt so sorry for him and looked forward to seeing him again.

Jason had a surprise for them. He asked Lionel to do him a huge favor. Please make plans to join your daughter at her home on July 16th. Then, don't show up because I will be showing up instead. I am coming a long way not to find her at home.

The Ackermans were delighted and said not to worry; they would make sure she was home.

Jason thanked them and said he was going to make an honest woman out of her again. They were beside themselves. Their grandson would now have his natural parents together.

***

Jason told the driver he could leave as he got out of the taxi. He walked up to the familiar front door and knocked. There was no answer. He knocked louder and still no answer.

He walked around the house. It was a beautiful day and Jason wondered if Maggie was still taking care of her flowers in the back yard.

As he turned the corner of the house he saw her, down on her knees with a large hat covering her head to block the sun and a spade in her hand shoveling the dirt over the freshly dug holes that she had filled with Petunias.

He silently crept toward her not wanting her to here his approach. He stepped up directly behind her and stopped.

"Whose girl are you?" he spoke softly.

Without turning around she raised her head, stopped

momentarily and then quietly replied ever so sternly,

"I'm your girl, Yank and don't YOU forget it.

END

About the Author

My life has included a journey across much of the world with sights and experiences that most people just read about. I always knew that I could tell a story on paper that would interest the reader, but delayed doing so while pioneering several business ventures and raising a family.

Life simply got in the way.

My love for literature persisted throughout my adult life and the need to express myself continued to follow me wherever life led me.

Over 96,000 people worldwide have read my published articles this year. That encouraged me to write my first novel.

I hope you enjoyed it. Watch for my next novel, Brothers Divided coming early 2017.

William Evans

Made in the USA
San Bernardino, CA
29 March 2017